CINDERELLA

An Adaptation of the Brothers Grimm Tale

Book by
W.A. Frankonis

Music by
Will Severin
and
George David Weiss

Lyrics by
George David Weiss

A SAMUEL FRENCH ACTING EDITION

SAMUEL FRENCH

FOUNDED 1830

New York Hollywood London Toronto

SAMUELFRENCH.COM

IMPORTANT BILLING AND CREDIT REQUIREMENTS

All producers of A TALE OF CINDERELLA *must* give credit to the Authors of the Work in all programs distributed in connection with performances of the Work, and in all instances in which the title of the Work appears for the purposes of advertising, publicizing or otherwise exploiting a production thereof, including, without limitation, programs, souvenir books and playbills. The names of the Authors must appear on a separate line in which no other matter appears, immediately following the title of the Work, and *must* be in size of type not less than 50% of the size used for the title of the Work.

Billing *must* be substantially as follows:

(NAME OF PRODUCER)

Presents

A Tale of Cinderella

Book by
W.A. FRANKONIS

Music by
WILL SEVERIN *and* GEORGE DAVID WEISS

Lyrics by
GEORGE DAVID WEISS

The New York State Theatre Institute's production of

A TALE OF
CINDERELLA

opened at the Schacht Fine Arts Center in Troy, New York
on December 4, 1994

Book by
W.A. Frankonis

Music by
Will Severin and George David Weiss

Lyrics by
George David Weiss

Setting by Richard Finkelstein

Costumes by Brent Griffin

Lighting by John McLain

Sound by Dan Toma

Orchestrations by Larry Moore

Musical Supervision and Dance Arrangements by
Dennis Buck

Vocal Direction and Vocal Arrangements by
Gary Aldrich

Conducted by Dennis Buck

Legal Counsel Floria V. Lasky
Music Preparation Emily Grishman Music Preparation

Production Stage Manager Heather Hazelton Hamelin

Choreographic Direction by Adrienne Spagnola Posner

Stage Direction by Patricia Di Benedetto Snyder

Co-produced for the New York State Theatre Institute by
Olga A. Delorey and Patricia Di Benedetto Snyder

Original Stage and Video Production Cast

Cinderella	Christianne Tisdale
Rafael the Gondolier	John McGuire
Prince Nicolo	Sean Frank Sullivan
Paolo	Joel Aroeste
Giametta	Mychelle Lee Vedder
Angelina (Cinderella as a child)	Catherine Wronowski
Pulchitruda	Erika Johnson Newell
Moltovoce	Joanne Lessner
Seppia	Margaret Robinson
La Stella	Lorraine Serabian
Il Compari	John Romeo
Peliculo	David Bunce

The Citizens of Venice Eileen Schuyler, Michael Steese, John Romeo, Sam Smith, Joel Aroeste, Laura Roth, John R. McEnerney, August J. Michaels, Etta Caren Fink, Jill Collins, Tony Hastings, Sarajane Brimhall, Mychelle Lee Vedder, David Bunce, Ward Dales, Mort Hess, Christopher Bessette, Vanessa Thorpe, Sam Smith and John Romeo

The Children of Venice Peter Kutchukian, Kerry Cronte, Dulcinea Vega Cuprill, Mathew O'Brien, Sarah Koblenz, Alyson Lange, Sean Mack and Dana Mainella

Keyboard	Mark Brockley and Graham Doig
Precussion	Joseph Conroy and Mark Foster
Trombone	William Meckley, Ken Olsen and Cathy Stone
Reeds	Paul Aldi

Original Cast / 2001 Tour

Cinderella	Michelle Dawson
Rafael the Gondolier	John McGuire
Prince Nícolo	Anthony Hastings
Paolo	Joel Aroeste
Giametta	Michaela Reilly
Angelina (Cinderella as a child)	Alyson Lange
Pulchitruda	Lynnie Godfrey
Moltovoce	Noëlle Gentile
Seppia	Mary Jane Hansen
La Stella	Lorraine Serabian
Il Compari	John Romeo
Peliculo	David Bunce

The Citizens of Venice
Michaela Reilly, 'Eileen

Schuyler, Michael Steese, Sarah Farnam, John R. McEnerney, Timothy Booth, Susan Cicarelli Caputo, Kerry Conte, Allan Snyder, Jessica Guyon, Ron Komora, David Gould, Byron Nilsson, Brandon Jones, Marva Ray and Mathew Stucky

The Children of Venice

Laura Kaiser, Dane Wilson, Alyson Lange, Meredith Anne Bull, Michelle Geisler, Ben Golub, Shannon Rafferty, Leslie Shrager and Whitney A. Wilson

ALSO AVAILABLE

Video, Original Cast CD & Vocal Selections
(Order directly from Samuel French, Inc.)

Study Guide* for use with *A Tale of Cinderella
(Order from The New York State Theatre Institute,
37 Front Street, Troy New York 12180)

MUSICAL NUMBERS

Act I

Musical Prologue	Cinderella and Voices
Buon Giorno	All Venetians
The Tale of Cinderella	Gondelier and Person
Hear Us	Both Angelinas and Paola
Cinderella	Chorus and/or Children
Poor, Poor, Poor	Moltovoce, Seppia and Pulchitruda
In the Air	Cinderella
These Graceful Hands	Paolo and Pulchitruda
Stepmother Casts a Spell	Pulchitruda and Paolo
Showoff	Moltovoce and Seppia
Have Faith	La Stella
Make Magic	Prince and Il Compari
Demons and Devils and Witches	Cinderella and Ensemble
Peliculo	Peliculo and Venetians
Unmarried Women	All Venetians

Act II

Out of the Ashes	Cinderella and Voices
Bring My Porridge	Pulchitruda, Moltovoce and Seppia
Some Sweet Day	Cinderella
Can You Believe It	Venetians
Love, Love, Love, Love	Cinderella and Paolo
Showoff (Reprise)	Moltovoce and Seppia
Bells / Mi Dispiace	Cinderella and Paolo
Amulet	Cinderella
Don't Mess with La Stella	La Stella
Be Back by Midnight	La Stella
Compliments	La Stella and Il Compari
No one Ever Told Me	Prince and Cinderella
The Prince	Children and Prince
I Am Your Bride, You Are My Love	Cinderella and Prince
Cinderella (Finale)	All Venetians

MAJOR CHARACTERS

CINDERELLA: This is a smart, responsible, attractive and loving young woman who is devoted to her father and the memory of her mother. While she is treated as a menial by her new step-relations, she is anything but menial in her heart and attitude. She puts up with them because this is her home and has been for a long time. She has a deep moral center but comes to see how even doing what is right is often a difficult choice. She is *not* the docile, vacant character typically portrayed as Cinderella.

PAOLO: Unlike in the original, the father has a more prominent role. He is a kindly, well-meaning soul who, after many years as a widower, has remarried, primarily because he doesn't want to be alone as he grows old. He loves his daughter deeply but in a largely ineffective way; he fails to protect her against the newcomers in their lives. While that failure is partly because of the spell his new wife has cast on him, he admirably comes to recognize and accept his responsibility for his daughter's lot.

PULCHITRUDA: The stepmother is best described as beauty cast in stone. She is scheming and pragmatic, and misuses the *amuleta díamore* to keep Paolo in line. To that extent, she has powers beyond the ordinary. Cold and largely unfeeling, she looms as Cinderella's major antagonist.

STEPSISTERS: For the most part, they are comic foils to Cinderella despite their troublesome ways toward her. The older, MOLTO-VOCE, is precisely what her name suggests: a loudmouth. The younger, SEPPIA, is learning the ways of her sister and mother, having little of her own character. Squid-like, as her name suggests, she takes bit of this and that to make herself.

LA STELLA: She is anything but the traditional fairy godmother. She *is* both godmother and grandmother to Cinderella, but she plays both roles with an attitude. Sharp, bright, feisty and uncommon, she uses the traditional wooden spoon as her magic wand — which has an attitude of its own — to stir up help or trouble, depending on the circumstances. Of equal importance in the course of events, she also finds love for herself, adding an element to the story which is not present in the original.

IL COMPARI: This new character is the Prince's godfather, and he comes almost wholebody out of the *commedia dell'arte*: the braggart soldier. Lively, boastful, comic and warm, he fumbles at making the wondrous happen with his sword (with an assist from La Stella). He also owns a romantic heart and a charm that attracts La Stella, thus leading them both to love late in their lives.

PRINCE: He is the fairly typical prince of the story, but even he is a more complete character than usual. He is warm and charming, but most important, he sees beyond the surface of things and takes matters of the heart seriously. He seeks not merely a bride but a soulmate with whom to make a life.

ACT I

(SCENE: An open square in Venice. Upstage, a canal before a back-drop of houses with shuttered windows. A bridge crossing the canal. At right, a structure that is a two-story revolve which at rise shows a wall and a balcony. Stairs lead from the up-center end of the balcony to the square. No windows, only a door in the face of the wall on the lower level. Perhaps a window or two show on the upper, balcony level.
Throughout the play, the action is broad and full of feeling. We are, after all, in Italy.
At rise, darkness and mist. Fingers of dawn beginning to creep in. Soft music underscores. The following song fragments are all ballad tempo at this point.)

VOICES.
COME UP FROM THE CELLAR ... CINDERELLA ....

(CINDERELLA leaves the house for the square. She carries a par-tially filled laundry basket which she sets down while she stretches and yawns.)

CINDERELLA. *(Softly.)*
BUON' GIORNO. GOOD MORNING ...

(She dances a few steps with the basket then goes up the stairs toward the bridge. Briefly, she watches the sun begin to rise.)

VOICES.
SHOW THE WORLD THAT UNDER ALL THOSE SMUDGES
YOU'RE *BELLA Ò.*

CINDERELLA. *(Softly.)*
HELLO MORNING, NEW DAY DAWNING ....

(A gondola appears with the GONDOLIER and the MASKED PAS-SENGER, who is the PRINCE returning from a masquerade after a long night, but he goes unrecognized. Without noticing, CIN-DERELLA goes off with the basket. ì Buonì Giornoì underscores lightly, tempo beginning to increase. Venetians begin to make appearances.)

MASKED PASSENGER. Why are you stopping here?

GONDOLIER. 'A moment's rest ... *and* it's a good place to begin the day, Signóre of the Mask, to feel life stirring again, a place of many stories. Listen ... you can hear them ....

(Noisy hustle and bustle of everyday activities in the square. A peddler with goods in yoked baskets, a fruit seller, bedding shaken out windows of the backdrop. CHILDREN playing. WOMAN with water jug balanced on her head.

Someone plays a concertina, and a MAN coaxes the water-jug WOMAN to dance. She tries to ignore him but her attempts to get around him become the dance itself and finally she joins in, all without removing the water jug from atop her head.)

NUN. *(With CHILDREN.)* Buon' giorno!

PAOLO. Buon' giorno, Bambini!

(CINDERELLA may reappear and participate during this segment, but must be back in the house by song's end and never prominent enough for the masked PRINCE to notice her.)

Song: *Buoní Giorno*

CHORUS.
BUONÍ GIORNO ... GOOD MORNING,
HOW ARE YOU? ... *COME ST¿ ?*
I'M FEELING VERY HAPPY —
HO-HO-HO ... HA-HA-HA!

GOOD MORNING ... *BUONÍ GIORNO*,
THE SUN IS HAPPY, TOO.
HE'S WEARING A GREAT BIG SMILE THAT SAYS,
"HOW DO YOU DO?"

BUONÍ GIORNO ... GOOD MORNING,
HOW ARE YOU? ... *COME ST¿ ?*
I'M FEELING SO FELICE *ó*
HO-HO-HO ... HA–HA–HA!

FA BEL TEMPO
IS PUTTING IT QUITE PRECISELY,
FA BEL TEMPO
THE WEATHER IS DOING NICELY, THANK YOU.
BUONÍ GIORNO .... GOOD MORNING,
HOW ARE YOU? ... *COME ST¿ ?*

I'M FEELING *MOLTO BUONO ó*
HO-HO-HO ... HA-HA-HA!

SKEPTICAL CITIZEN.
BUT ...
OF COURSE ...
IT IS VERY *POSSIBLE*
THAT THE WEATHER COULD SUDDENLY CHANGE,
THAT THE SUN COULD HIDE BEHIND DARK, DARK CLOUDS
AND THINGS COULD ALL FEEL STRANGE.
WHEN THE DAY BECOMES GLUM AND GLOOMY,
BLACK MAGIC IS UNFURLED.
THAT'S WHEN EVIL SPRITS RULE THE WORLD!

STALWART CITIZEN.
WE HAVE TO BE STRONG,
TAKE A FIRM STANCE,
WE'LL GIVE THE BAD GUYS A KICK IN THE PANTS,
SO ...

ALL.
BUONí GIORNO ... GOOD MORNING,
HOW ARE YOU? ... *COME ST¿ ?*
I'M FEELING VERY HAPPY, SO *FELICE, MOLTO BUONO*
PIZZICATO, MOZZARELLA, PARMIGIANA, CALAMARI,
    ANTIPASTO AND
SPAGHETTI! HO-HO-HO! HEE-HEE-HEE!
HEH-HEH-HEH, HOO-HOO-HOO, HEY-HEY-HEY
HA-HA-HA!

*(Music underscores. Someone in the square notices the gondola and
    calls out.)*

    PERSON. Hey ... Rafael ... why the long puss? You make your
passenger cry and get his beautiful party mask all wet ...
    PERSON. ... and he won't give you a little extra for your trou-
ble.
    PERSON. Why don't you sing like the other gondoliers in Ven-
ice? Make the signóre happy?
    PERSON. *Basta!* A sad story needs a long face.
    PERSON. You're always telling sad stories!
    PERSON. Which one today ...?
    PERSON. ... the brave soldier who never returned to his young
wife ...?
    PERSON. ... or poor Rafael, the gondolier who needs *lira* for
wine at *la taverna!*

(Mocking laughter.)

GONDOLIER. *Silenzio!* Be respectful! I intend to tell of Giametta and Paola.

(The crowd quiets and sobers.)

CROWD. O-o-oh ... the saddest tale of all.

(They decide to join in the storytelling in a mix of dialog and opera falsa.)

PERSON. A tale to make an opera of, signóre ...
PERSON. ... and *e-e-e-everyone* would weep.
GONDOLIER. The greatest tales *always* make you weep, signóre, while their beauty makes your heart swell with happiness and love. Like life, *dolorŮsa ma molto bĔllo.*
PASSENGER. Who is it you speak of? Why is their tale the saddest of all?

(As people gather near the gondola, light shifts, and they are shadowed while the square takes on the golden sepia of memory where the GONDOLIERĹs tale is enacted.)

GONDOLIER.
THEY WERE PAOLO ...
    PERSON.
... THE WEALTHY MERCHANT ...
    PERSON.
... AND HIS WIFE

    PERSON. *(Spoken.)* ... Giametta ...

    PERSON.
... WITH MIDNIGHT IN HER HAIR.
    PERSON.
HOW THEY LOVED THEIR PRECIOUS CHILD ...
    GONDOLIER.
... ANGELINA ... ANGELINA ...

(PAOLO dances into the square with ANGELINA, an extravagant waltz. GIAMETTA watches and applauds. PAOLO bows to ANGELINA, waves, exits.)

GONDOLIER. And when Paolo sailed away ...
PERSON. ... mother and daughter waited.

(ANGELINA runs to GIAMETTA and takes her cap and puts it on. It is much too large. GIAMETTA straightens the cap on the child.)

GIAMETTA. Don't be sad, child, your poppa always comes back from his voyages. Here ... you wear the amulet he gave me to remember him by. And every night, we'll sing to him far away at sea — until he returns ... *si?*
ANGELINA. *Si,* Mommá.

(She adjusts the amulet, and they go into the house. On the drop a ship is mistily suggested in the distance.)

GONDOLIER. And always they were waiting when Paolo returned ...

PERSON.
UNTIL THAT SAD, UNHAPPY DAY ...

(ANGELINA appears in the square.)

PERSON. ... when only Angelina met poor Paolo in the square ...

(ANGELINA runs to PAOLO and throws herself, sobbing, into his arms.)

PERSON.
... THE LOVELY GIAMETTA ...

GONDOLIER. The fever, signor, it took her as it did so many that winter.

PERSON.
... THE LOVELY GIAMETTA WAS NO MORE.

(A bell tolls funereally. In the air, hushed voices hover, speaking only the name, i Giametta.i While PAOLO and ANGELINA climb to the balcony, the voices back the dialog and grow progressively fainter until disappearing altogether. i Hear Usi begins as underscore.)

GONDOLIER. Child and husband were alone ...
PAOLO. Don't cry, child ... we'll remember her. You have her cap and ....
ANGELINA. ... and *you* take the amulet, Poppa, 'til Momma comes back.
PAOLO. It was my heart, I told her, for safekeeping. Thank you, cara mia, but Mommá is not on a voyage one day to return. She's

gone to live in the stars. We'll see her every night and sing to her ...
just as you and she did when I was gone at sea. Did you know I heard
you?

ANGELINA. You *really* did?

PAOLO. *Si* ... angel voices. Come, we'll sing now ... but sing
loud, it's a *long* way.

GONDOLIER. Their voices often rose to the lovely Giametta
in the stars. And through the years, father and daughter never forgot
her.

*(During the song, light fades on the child ANGELINA and rises on the
grown ANGELINA/CINDERELLA. Perhaps there is a distance
between the two that calls for PAOLO to move to the older to
help the sense of a passage of years. An identical cap on the
grown daughter should help to identify her.)*

Song: *Hear Us*

PAOLO and BOTH ANGELINAS.
HEAR US, HEAR US,
THO' YOU'RE FAR AWAY;
HEAR THE SONG THAT I SEND
BEYOND THE RAINBOW'S END.
HEAR US, HEAR US,
THROUGH BLUE SKIES OR GREY;
HEAR EACH BEAT OF OUR HEARTS,
THAT'S WHERE THE MUSIC STARTS.
IF I FLY TO THE MOON, CAN I REACH YOU?
IF I STAND ON A STAR, CAN WE TOUCH?
WAY UP HIGH ON A CLOUD,
WILL MY EYES BE ALLOWED
TO SEE THE SMILE I MISS SO MUCH?

HEAR US, HEAR US,
AS TIME PASSES BY,
IT CAN NEVER ERASE
THE MEMORY OF YOUR FACE.
WE STILL LOVE YOU,
WE STILL NEED YOU,
CAN'T YOU HEAR
THE WAY OUR HEARTS STILL CRY.

*(Light fades on PAOLO and ANGELINA/CINDERELLA. All are lost
in thought. Scene returns to the normal light of day as the square
empties, VENETIANS going about their business.)*

PASSENGER. What happened to Angelina ... and to Paolo?

GONDOLIER. Ah ... she grew up ... *molta bËlla* ... so beautiful ... the *exact* image of her mother. And Paolo ...

PERSON. ... he grew up, too ... fat and prosperous ...

PERSON. ... the *exact* image of a rich merchant!

PASSENGER. So the tale has a happy ending ... they lived happily ever after!

GONDOLIER. Ah ... well ... they live in Venice still, true ... Angelina all grown up as I said ... but happily ...? Who knows? She has a hard life now, with a stepmother and stepsisters. Her story is not yet finished, signóre, so come, I have another story with an ending that will make you laugh ....

(Light shifts, losing gondola entirely as it poles off. Music segues into ì Cinderellaî theme as the balcony revolves partway to reveal a lower level interior. A kitchen with hearth, table and chairs, pots and pans on the wall. An invisible downstage ì doorî from kitchen to square. In the hearth, CINDERELLA is scrubbing, back to audience.
During the revolve, the music of the ì Cinderellaî theme underscores, and voices off sing.)

Song: *Cinderella*

CHORUS and/or CHILDREN.
COME UP FROM THE CELLAR, CINDERELLA,
SHOW THE WORLD THAT UNDER ALL THOSE SMUDGES
YOU'RE *BELLA*.
WARM THE SUN,
BREATHE SWEET WORDS
TO THE BREEZE,
ONE BY ONE
CHARM THE BIRDS
OFF THE TREES.

PULCHITRUDA. *(Off and strident.)* ANGEL-I-I-I-INA!

(Commotion off. Shouts and shrieking laughter. Enter PULCHI-TRUDA along with her daughters, the mercurial MOLTOVOCE and the mousy SEPPIA.)

MOLTOVOCE. Mother ... if you call her that, she won't come. That's her real name, not a servant's name ... *she* says.

SEPPIA. So if you want our *servant*, you have to call her ...

MOLTOVOCE and **SEPPIA.** CIN-N-DER-EL-L-L-LA!

PULCHITRUDA. I will call her as I wish ... and she will answer if she knows what's good for her. COME HERE, YOU LAZY GIRL!

(She tugs CINDERELLA, in tattered, soot-covered clothes, from the hearth, pulling off her shoe in the process. The stepsisters shriek with laughter.)

MOLTOVOCE. You see ... she looks like *la cenerÉntola Ö* a Cinderella ...
    SEPPIA. ... not an Angelina!
    CINDERELLA. Yes, Pulchitruda?
    PULCHITRUDA. Stepmother.
    CINDERELLA. Yes, stepmother. I'm here.
    PULCHITRUDA. No ... signóra.
    CINDERELLA. I'm here, signóra.
    MOLTOVOCE. Ooh-ooh ... and all me Signorina Moltovoce the beautiful!
    SEPPIA. And me, Signorina Seppia the beautifuller!
    CINDERELLA. Ah yes, beauty like the foul water people throw in the canals.
    MOLTOVOCE and **SEPPIA.** Oh ... mother! She insulted us! Pinch her cheeks, Mother! Yell at her!

(PULCHITRUDA pinches.)

    PULCHITRUDA. But I leave the yelling to her father. Right now ....

(She drags an oversized laundry basket to the center of the room.)

    MOLTOVOCE and **SEPPIA.** Oh ... laundry day! We love laundry day! It's so much fun!

(They toss laundry around and draw a hat from the basket.)

    CINDERELLA. That's my mother's!
    PAOLO. Here ... here! What is this? What's happening?
    MOLTOVOCE and **SEPPIA.** Stepfather!
    MOLTOVOCE. You're back!
    SEPPIA. You're back!
    MOLTOVOCE. I just said that.

(SEPPIA sulks.)

    PULCHITRUDA. So, Paolo, did the voyage go well?

(PAOLO helps CINDERELLA up.)

PAOLO. Not so well this time. What is it, my child? What happened? And your momma's old hat ....

CINDERELLA. It's laundry day, Poppa.

PULCHITRUDA. What do you mean ... husband ... not so well this time?

PAOLO. Not so well is what I mean. I lost two ships to a storm. A great deal of money at the bottom of the sea.

PULCHITRUDA. Leaving us ...?

PAOLO. ... with not so much money as before.

SEPPIA. POOR?

MOLTOVOCE. P-o-o-o-or? We can't be ...

Song: Poor, Poor, Poor

MOLTOVOCE and **SEPPIA.**
POOR, POOR, POOR.
WE'RE MUCH TOO GOOD TO BE POOR.
MOMMA, YOU PROMISED WE WOULDN'T BE, COULDN'T BE
    SHOULDN'T BE ...
POOR, POOR, POOR. *(Sigh.)*
GEMS AND PEARLS *(Sob.)*
PLEASE KEEP THEM ALIVE IN OUR WORLD *(Big sob.)*
YOU VOWED THAT POVERTY ... NEVER WOULD, NEVER
    COULD, *NEVER SHOULD* ...
REACH YOUR GIRLS!

IT'S MUCH, TOO MUCH OF A SACRIFICE
TO NEED TO WEAR THE SAME DRESS TWICE.
MOMMA, MOMMA, TELL US, PLEASE,
WE WON'T HAVE TO LIVE IN A DITCH,
THAT SOON WE'LL WAKE
FROM THE HORRIBLE NIGHTMARE
AND STILL BE RICH *(Sobs.)* NOT ...
POOR, POOR, POOR.
WE'RE MUCH TOO GOOD TO BE POOR.

PULCHITRUDA. *(Spoken:)*
Being poor is only for the poor,
Not for elegant people like us.
Why do the poor have to make such a fuss?
Just because they don't have money?

MOLTOVOCE and **SEPPIA.** *(Spoken:)*
That's funny. *(Sung:)*
IF HE CAN'T CORRECT THIS ALIEN SITUATION ...
     PULCHITRUDA. *(Spoken:)*
... Arriverdérci, former husband.
     MOLTOVOCE and **SEPPIA.** *(Sung:)*
WE'RE LEAVING ON A MEDITERRANEAN VACATION.

     PAOLO. Enough uproar. No one will starve! Less wealth, less care.
     PULCHITRUDA. I remind you why you married me.
     PAOLO. Palermo's most beautiful woman to grace my household ... yes.
     PULCHITRUDA. And beauty belongs with wealth ... *and* with the *amuleto diamÛre.*
     PAOLO. Yes ,.. not the wisest thing I've ever said ... *(He fights off the slight flicker of the amulet.)* ... but my daughter. Why ... so dirty as if cleaning the hearth?
     PULCHITRUDA. Someone must do the work ... if we are to be poor.
     PAOLO. Angelina ... she ... ?
     PULCHITRUDA. ... insulted *my* daughters, threatened to throw them in the canal.
     SEPPIA. In the foulest canal, she said!
     MOLTOVOCE. With the chamber pots, she said.
     PAOLO. My Angelina, did you ...?
     CINDERELLA. Poppa, I didn't. I only said ....
     PULCHITRUDA. She is a sharp, ungrateful girl, husband, and needs a firm hand. I won't have her misbehave and laze around the house while we put up with less than we bargained for....
     PAOLO. Leave me alone with her. Please, Pulchitruda ... I will talk with her. *(PULCHITRUDA concedes but as she and the STEP-SISTERS exit, she raises a warning finger at PAOLO.)* What is it, daughter? Tell me.
     CINDERELLA. What's to say, Poppa? There is much work to do, and Pulchitruda is your ... new ... wife, and I ...
     PAOLO. ... and you are a good girl who tries to do good things.
     CINDERELLA. Because it is *our* house, Poppa! *Ours* and ...

(PAOLO draws CINDERELLA to the square. He takes the cap from her and studies it as a memory.)

     PAOLO. ... and your momma's. Yes, I still miss her, too. *(Pause.)* I will talk to Pulchitruda. I will say to help out and ....
     CINDERELLA. No! Then it will only be worse! They do not know about work. What they clean, I would only have to do over.

PAOLO. Then ... what?

CINDERELLA. Stay home more. We're *not* poor ... only in money. Oh, Poppa, why did you ...?

PAOLO. ... marry her? It's not good to be alone as you grow old.

CINDERELLA. Poppa ... in the marketplace ... they say Pulchitruda is a witch. I heard them! And she has cast a spell on you!

(PAOLO laughs at the idea.)

PAOLO. They also say your GodMama is a witch ... and there they may be right. But do you believe superstitions? People talk, *cara mia*, say things true or not.

CINDERELLA. But there *is* magic in life, Poppa ... good magic ... and bad magic.

PAOLO. Who told you this? The old gypsy ... Signóra Olganna?

CINDERELLA. No-o-o ... GodMama.

PAOLO. Ah ... of course ... *la strega Ö*

(He mimes a wicked witch.)

CINDERELLA. ... and Mommá.

PAOLO. Oh. *(He puts the cap back on her.)* You look so much like her ... I wish ... we could have been happy, the three of us ... so sad.

CINDERELLA. Happiness always comes back Poppa. You'll see.

PAOLO. Yes? Will you go to the market and bring a basketful?

CINDERELLA. We only have to breathe.

PAOLO. You believe that, Angelina ... when they call you Cinderella?

CINDERELLA. Well ... sometimes there are storms ... thunder and lightning ... but yes, I *must* believe it, especially when ...

Song: In the Air

CINDERELLA.
IN THE MIDST OF DARK AND DREARY HOURS,
WHEN IT SEEMS THAT GARDENS WILL NO LONGER GROW
       THEIR FLOWERS
HOW I WISH THAT I COULD HEAR
A DIFFERENT KIND OF SOUND
SOMETHING THAT WILL LIFT ME UP
INSTEAD OF TEAR ME DOWN.

THEN A SECRET VOICE
TURNS MY HEART AROUND,
IT WHISPERS: LISTEN, YOU CAN HEAR IT
FLOATING IN THE AIR,
HAPPINESS IS SINGING
EVERYWHERE '

LISTEN TO THE CHILDREN,
SOUNDS YOU CAN'T ERASE,
HAPPINESS IS POURING FORTH FROM EVERY FACE.
YOU CAN ALMOST TOUCH IT,
HOLD IT IN YOUR HAND,
ALMOST FEEL IT CHASING
EVERY CARE.
AND EVERY HEART THAT HAS A LOT OF LOVE TO GIVE
HELPS ANOTHER LONELY HEART TO LIVE.
THAT'S HAPPINESS, THAT'S HAPPINESS.
AND IT'S THERE
IN THE AIR
EVERYWHERE
IN THE AIR —
LISTEN!

HEAR IT BRUSH AGAINST YOUR CHEEK,
HEAR IT SHIMMER IN YOUR HAIR,
SOUNDS OF HAPPINESS CAN SPEAK
ANY PLACE, ANYWHERE,
SO WHILE GOING ON YOUR WAY, STOP
A HUNDRED TIMES A DAY,
STOP
AND LISTEN VERY WELL AND TAKE DEEP BREATHS,
YOU'LL BE UNDERNEATH THE SPELL OF HAPPINESS ...
IN THE AIR
IN THE AIR
IN THE AIR
IN THE AIR
THE SOUND OF HAPPINESS,
THE SOUND OF HAPPINESS
IS IN THE AIR. '

PULCHITRUDA. *(Off.)* Cinder-el-l-la!
PAOLO. Hah ... thunder and lightning ... eh? I don't like them calling you that.
CINDERELLA. It doesn't matter, Poppa, because I know who I am. If I am *una cenerEntola* to them, then I will be Cinderella proudly. It won't change what's inside.

(PAOLO embraces her.)

>PAOLO. You have the courage ...
>CINDERELLA. ... of a merchant sailor who dares the sea.
>PAOLO. ... of your mother. She would be happy about you.

(Entering, PULCHITRUDA hears.)

>PULCHITRUDA. And I would be happy if the laundry were tended. The day almost gone and barely half your chores done.
>CINDERELLA. Yes, stepmother, right away.
>PAOLO. *(Irony.)* In the air?
>CINDERELLA. Breathe!

(She lugs the basket off.)

>PAOLO. Pulchitruda ... there's no need for a sharp tongue ... a little caring and sympathy ....
>PULCHITRUDA. *She* owns the sharp tongue — lacks respect, takes liberties ....
>PAOLO. No ... she is *good.* You ... this ... it's all new for her ... *and* us ... a little time to get used to new ways ....
>PULCHITRUDA. She would drive a wedge between us ... *your* daughter.
>PAOLO. Scaring a bird is not the way to catch it. Do your share ... along with your daughters ....
>PULCHITRUDA. Turn these hands to ordinary work?
>PAOLO. I know ... so soft, so smooth ....

Song: Stepmother Casts a Spell

PULCHITRUDA.
WHEN I ASK YOU DO YOU LOVE ME,
IS THE ANSWER YES?
>**PAOLO.**
YES.

PULCHITRUDA.
DARE I THINK YOU WANT TO PLEASE ME?
IS THE ANSWER YES.
>**PAOLO.**
YES.

PULCHITRUDA.
DO YOU WANT TO MAKE ME HAPPY?

IS THE ANSWER YES?
>   **PAOLO.**
YES.

>   **PULCHITRUDA.**
THEN I'M SURE YOU'LL LEAVE YOUR DAUGHTER
IN MY VERY TENDER HANDS ... YES?
>   **PAOLO.**
YES, BUT ...
>   **PULCHITRUDA.**
OH, NO. HUSBAND, NO BUTS ... ONLY YES!
>   **PAOLO.**
YES.

> **PULCHITRUDA.** Then come, I will bathe you after your long voyage ... refresh you so you can insist on the best price for what goods are not at the bottom of the sea.

> *(They exit. Light restores. MOLTOVOCE and SEPPIA enter, obviously having eavesdropped.)*

> **MOLTOVOCE.** Mother has her mysterious ways.
> **SEPPIA.** Fat good it does *us*! Oh, Moltovoce, we're so BEAU-U-U-TIFUL ... but no party invitations again! It's BO-O-ORING! What can we do?
> **MOLTOVOCE.** Make Cinderella miserable
> **SEPPIA.** She's washing the laundry.
> **MOLTOVOCE.** Yes, we can ... help her.
> **SEPPIA.** Help? With these ... *graceful* ... hands!
> **MOLTOVOCE.** No, fishflesh ... wake up! Help her make it a-a-al-ll dirty again!

> *(Revolve returns to outside. CINDERELLA appears with the laundry basket on her hip and CHILD in hand. Other CHILDREN tag along.)*

> **CHILD.** Tell us a story, Cinderella!
> **CINDERELLA.** Ah ... a story ... how about the Blind Woman and the Prince?
> **CHILDREN.** *Si, si*!
> **CINDERELLA.** *(Donning a blindfold.)* Once upon a time, there 'as a blind woman ...

> *'TEPSISTERS onto the balcony.)*

> **SEPPIA.** Look ... there she is! Telling stories because she thinks

the children like her.

Song: Showoff

MOLTOVOCE and **SEPPIA.**
SHOWOFF,
SHE'S JUST A SHOWOFF,
STUPID CINDERELLA IS A SHOWOFF.
WHAT HAS SHE GOT TO BOAST ABOUT?
WHERE ON THE SCALE DOES SHE RATE?
WHY DOES SHE STAND IN THE SQUARE AND SHOUT,
"LOOK, EV'REYBODY, I'M GREAT!"?

BIG SHOT, SHE'S SUCH A BIG SHOT.
I DON'T KNOW WHAT MAKES HER THINK
SHE'S SO HOT.
FORCING THE KIDS TO HANG AROUND,
TWISTING THEIR ARMS TO STAY.
PRACTICALLY KNOCKING THEM TO THE GROUND,
ORDERING THEM TO PLAY. JUST BECAUSE SHE'S
        BEAUTIFUL,
JUST BECAUSE SHE'S SMART,
JUST BECAUSE SHE'S TALENTED
AND HAS A TENDER HEART,
JUST BECAUSE WHEN SHE WALKS BY,
WEEPIN' WILLOWS SMILE,
CROWS BEGIN TO SIGH,
AND THE TAILS OF LITTLE DOGGIES WAG,
IS THAT ANY REASON TO BRAG?
SHE'S A SHOWOFF,
A SHOWOFF,
SHE'S JUST A SHOWOFF,
A SHOWOFF ––
STUPID CINDERELLA IS A SHOWOFF!

WHY DENY THAT SOONER OR LATER
I'LL HAVE TO TELL HER
THAT I HATE HER!

*(The STEPSISTERS sneak up on CINDERELLA. Spotting them, the
CHILDREN quiet fearfully and draw away from the game after
being warned by the STEPSISTERS to say nothing Ö or else.)*

CINDERELLA. ... and so the blind woman could see ... in her
heart ... and she and the prince lived happily ever after. *(The STEP-*

SISTERS maneuver into place. CINDERELLA senses something from the sudden quiet. She halts uncertainly, giving the STEPSISTERS the opportunity to position themselves.) Children? Are you hiding on me? Gabriella? Santoro? Oh, you little devils are trying to trick me! Vincenzo ... where are you?

(She waits, listens, becomes concerned and starts to doff the blindfold.)

CHILDREN. Cinderella ... watch out!

(The STEPSISTERS strike, MOLTOVOCE pushing CINDERELLA over the kneeling SEPPIA. The laundry flies everywhere. CINDERELLA doffs the blindfold and leaps to her feet.)

CINDERELLA. You two!

(CINDERELLA grabs MOLTOVOCE, drags her upstage, and tosses her into the canal.
She grabs SEPPIA and does the same. STEPSISTERS emerge sopping wet to jeers and laughter from the children and run off squealing and wringing each other out. VOICES call to the CHILDREN.)

VOICES. Andi‡mo! Mangi‡mo!
CINDERELLA. Run along Rita ... do not keep your happy dinner waiting. Eat well ... sleep deep ... dream happy. *(CHILDREN scatter, leaving CINDERELLA alone. She goes to the laundry and begins to gather it.)* Soiled again! Pulchituda will blame me. *(She slumps unhappily on a heap of newly dirtied laundry. She removes the cap and holds it.)* Oh, Momma ... I wish you were still here! Poor Poppa ... I'm sure he's bewitched. Why else would he marry someone so unlike you? Make himself so unhappy?
(In the evening air, a voice, that of the godmother LA STELLA.)

LA STELLA. And you, child ... aren't you unhappy too?
CINDERELLA. GodMama?
LA STELLA. Eh ... who else? Who loves you but La Stella? Aside from you stubborn father, that is?
CINDERELLA. You, GodMama. But where are you?
LA STELLA. *Pazienza Ö pazienza Ö* I'm hurrying. My voice goes like a rabbit, but this old gondola like a turtle. So answer, aren't you ...?
CINDERELLA. Unhappy, too ... yes.
LA STELLA. Then why think *only* of your father? Like your momma, you always put others first.
CINDERELLA. If she were here, it would be different.

LA STELLA. Sure ... but she isn't, so you have me ... the same thing.

CINDERELLA. Almost.

LA STELLA. No, the same. Wait ... one more spoonful of moonlight and ... here comes La Stella! *(A self-propelled gondola appears with LA STELLA, a slow-moving, wrinkled figure ó* vecchia come il cucco *ó as old as the hills.)* A-ah ... all caught up to my voice. *(They exchange a kiss.)* So ... I am your *nonna* before I am your GodMama ... *non Évero?*

CINDERELLA. Yes ... it's true.

LA STELLA. And so, because your momma came from me, she is *always* in me, so we are the same person ... simple, eh?

CINDERELLA. Yes, but, *Nonna* ... what's to be done for Poppa ... *and* for me, too? He won't send these troublemakers away.

LA STELLA. No ... but one door shuts and another opens.

CINDERELLA. Sounds like ... small hope to me, GodMama.

LA STELLA. Happiness is in the air.

CINDERELLA. Well ... for Poppa's sake I say that, but ....

Song: Have Faith

LA STELLA. *(Spoken.)* ... it *is* there, child ... sh-h-h ... if you let yourself ... *(Sings:)*
HAVE FAITH, BELIEVE THAT DREAMS COME TRUE..
AND IF YOU WILL, I PROMISE YOU,
THERE'S NOTHING ON THIS EARTH
YOU CAN'T ACHIEVE.
THE STARS ARE CLOSER THAN YOU THINK.
YOU'RE STANDING RIGHT AT AT THE BRINK.
THE WORLD IS YOURS
IF YOU HAVE FAITH,
IF YOU BELIEVE.

CINDERELLA. Faith in what? I look ahead and see only ....

LA STELLA. *(Spoken.)* What? Open *these* eyes ... here ... in your heart, then ... *(Sings:)*
THE STARS ARE CLOSER THAN YOU THINK
YOU'RE STANDING RIGHT AT AT THE BRINK.

EACH MISTY RAINBOW YOU EVER CHASED
EACH SWEET ADVENTURE YOU LONG TO TASTE
IS THERE JUST WAITING TO BE EMBRACED.
HAVE FAITH, YOU'LL FIND YOUR DREAM
IF YOU HAVE FAITH,
IF YOU BELIEVE.

CINDERELLA. Oh, *Nonna*, I try, but ...
IL COMPARI. *(Offstage.)* I was in Sicily then ....
LA STELLA. Sh-h-h. Someone's coming. *Un bandito*, maybe.
Hide in the shadows. I will stay near, but like a dark wall!

(Arms outstretched, back to the audience, she becomes a ı wall.î IL COMPARI, the' GodPapa, enters with the PRINCE, the latter in costume and full mask.)

IL COMPARI. So there I am ... surrounded by at least a hundred brigands ... *(He draws his sword.) Sta guardia,* Godson, someone is ... hide in the shadows! Who's there? Speak up or I'll run you through. Answer!
LA STELLA. What makes you the boss, eh?
IL COMPARI. Me? It's my job to be the boss!
LA STELLA. You look more like ...

Song: Insults
[translations bracketed]

LA STELLA.	
ZAMPOGNA!	[windbag]
IL COMPARI.	
LA STREGA!	[witch]
LA STELLA.	
ELEFANTE!	[elephant]
IL COMPARI.	
VULCANO!	[volcano]
LA STELLA.	
CAFÒNE!	[vulgar person]
IL COMPARI.	
SERPE IN SENO!	[snake in the grass]
BOTH.	

BAH! A THOUSAND INSULTS ON YOUR HEAD!

IL COMPARI. So ... now that we've met, good evening, signóra.

(IL COMPARI doffs his hat, bows.)

LA STELLA. And you ... *buona sera* to you, signóre ... and you are?
IL COMPARI. Il Compari, the GodPapa.
LA STELLA. Don Compari? Ah-hah ... my husband, Don Giacomo Volpe ... rest his soul ... told me of you.

IL COMPARI. Don Volpe, eh? I remember. And *you*? No insult intended, but ... you looked like a wall.

LA STELLA. Me? I am La Stella, only a GodMama of a little angel ... not a big boss like you. Only one boss at a time, eh?

IL COMPARI. *Sí*, one boss ... brave, bold, fearless, protector of the innocent, an expert swordsman —— exactly like IL COMPARI, THE ...

(LA STELLA has had enough.)

LA STELLA. Mommá mia ... what a line!

IL COMPARI. What?

LA STELLA. Look out! Behind you! *Un drago! Addío* for now, my child.

(She disappears.)

IL COMPARI. There's no dragon ... where is she? Where did she go?

(PRINCE comes forward.)

PRINCE. Who?

IL COMPARI. Who? Why, that ... great monster! Eight arms! Fingers like scimitars! Eyes like lightning, a tongue like ....

PRINCE. I saw no monster, GodPapa.

IL COMPARI. Then I frightened her ... *it* ... off, me and my trusty blade and the fierce reputation of ... the GodPapa, Il Compari!

PRINCE. Leaving behind her laundry?

IL COMPARI. Ah ... well ... even monsters need clean clothes.

(PRINCE moves toward the scattered laundry, spots CINDERELLA, halts.)

PRINCE. Oh ... *saluto*, signorina ... I did not see you there.

CINDERELLA. I blend with the night. It is the soot from cleaning the hearth.

PRINCE. And your laundry ... cleaning the hearth, too?

CINDERELLA. My laundry ... *was* clean, now it is not.

PRINCE. And it is too late to clean it again.

CINDERELLA. Yes. The washhouse is closed.

PRINCE. Then let me help you gather it.

CINDERELLA. Oh, no, signóre, you'll dirty your costume.

PRINCE. If it wins me a smile like the one I think lurks behind the smudge on you face, then .... *(CINDERELLA scrubs at her face, but makes the smudge worse. The PRINCE teases.)* Ah ... *much* better ... but perhaps ... *mi permetto? (He cleans the smudge with a handkerchief.)* There. Now a smile, too? *(CINDERELLA smiles at him.)* Look, GodPapa ... a smile like thousands and thousands of stars!

(IL COMPARI gestures they should be leaving.)

CINDERELLA. Oh ... signóre ... you make flattering words, but ....
PRINCE. No ... *Évero.* Your smile ... it glows with ....

(He sees she is uncomfortable with his extravagance and stops. He helps her gather the laundry into the basket as IL COMPARI decides to take forty winks.)

CINDERELLA. You are kind, signóre ... to help a stranger gather her laundry.
PRINCE. Laundry makes friends of strangers ...
CINDERELLA. That's true! At the washhouse, I ... oh, that's not how you mean.
PRINCE. ... and you have so *much* laundry, we will be *good* friends.
CINDERELLA. Do you always make friends this way?

(They share a laugh.)

PRINCE. Sometimes real ... friends ... are not easy to find ... or keep.
CINDERELLA. How sad, signóre ... but I know what you mean.
PRINCE. Truly?
CINDERELLA. Yes ... but if *everyone* were so helpful and kind ... then ....

(He hands her the last piece, but then doesn't let go of it.)

PRINCE. Now we are friends ... will you tell me your name?
CINDERELLA. Oh, no, signóre ... it would not be proper.
PRINCE. Then your mother taught you the old ways.

(IL COMPARI jolts awake.)

IL COMPARI. A-a-h ... the old ways. The old ways are best. Why when I was young, and a beautiful *signorina* ...
PRINCE. Not now, GodPapa. I must escort *this* signorina home ... keep her safe from ... monsters with eight arms and ...
CINDERELLA. Please, signóre, no. Thank you for helping, but ...

PRINCE. No trouble, I ...
CINDERELLA. I *will* be safe.
PRINCE. Then one more smile. At least that.

(CINDERELLA smiles and pulls away. From the darkness, she calls back.)

CINDERELLA. I hope you enjoy your party ... and find a friend.
PRINCE. I already have! And your beautiful smile ... it *does* glow like stars ... Signorina Whoever-You-Are! Thank you for lending it to me. *(Humming a tune to be heard later at the ball, he dances with a piece of laundry left behind unseen.)* Ah ... GodPapa! I am in love!
IL COMPARI. What ... with a piece of laundry?
PRINCE. With starlight!
IL COMPARI. Ah ... how can a prince love a laundress? All those princesses ....
PRINCE. *Sì* ... exactly the problem! GodPapa ... the world has beautiful women of good hearts. Why must I, Prince of Venice, choose from dull, spoiled princesses who know only money and jewels ... and feel nothing but their own greed?
IL COMPARI. The King ... wants only the best for you.
PRINCE. From what he *offers* ... not what my heart wants! Like the signorina who was here ... an angel. GodPapa, help ... a little miracle!

Song: Make Magic

PRINCE.
MY HEART IS HEAVY, MY SOUL IS SAD.
I'VE BEEN COMPLAINING TO THE KING, MY DAD,
"I WANT TO FALL IN LOVE SO BADLY."
(Spoken.) "But with whom ... a broom?"
A WARM AND TENDER HAND TO HOLD LIKE THIS.
(Spoken.) Especially when the weather starts getting cold.
I WANT TO FIND SOMEONE WHO'LL MISS ME.
(Spoken.) Oh, please, COMPARI, I know you can do it.

MAKE MAGIC, MAKE MAGIC,
DO IMPOSSIBLE THINGS.
MAKE MANDOLINS PLAY
THEIR BEAUTIFUL SONGS
EVEN WITH NO STRINGS.
MAKE EGGPLANTS GROW IN THE ICE AND SNOW,
MAKE THE SUN COME OUT AT NIGHT.

IMPROVE YOUR SKILL,
KEEP DOING IT 'TIL
YOU'RE DOING IT RIGHT.

MAKE MAGIC, MAKE MAGIC,
PLEASE DON'T LET ME DOWN.
MAKE MY PAIN AND HEARTACHE TAKE
A QUICK TRIP OUT OF TOWN.

IL COMPARI. *(Spoken.) Magic?* Hah! It's not like just snapping your fingers, you know. But, of course, if I *wanted* to ... why I could .... *(Sung.)*
MAKE MAGIC, MAKE MAGIC,
DO INCREDIBLE TRICKS.
MAKE WALRUSES FLY 'WAY OVER THE SKY,
MAKE A CAT HAVE CHICKS.
MAKE MONKEYS TALK WITH AN IRISH BROGUE,
MAKE DRAGONS RUN AND HIDE.
I'LL PRACTICE WELL EACH MAGICAL SPELL
I EVER HAVE TRIED.

MAKE MAGIC, MAKE MAGIC
USE AMULETS AND CHARMS.
I'LL WAVE MY SWORD AND FIND YOUR LOVE,
AND FILL YOUR EMPTY ARMS.
(Spoken.) Is that what you mean? Magic like that?

PRINCE. *(Spoken.)* Yes! *(Sung.)*
MAKE MAGIC, MAKE MAGIC,
DO UNDOABLE DEEDS.
    IL COMPARI.
MAKE OSTRICHES SQUEEZE SPAGHETTI AND CHEESE
OUT OF PUMPKIN SEED.
    PRINCE.
MAKE ICE CREAM FLOW FROM A VOLCANO ...
    IL COMPARI.'
MAKE A LAKE OF CHOCOLATE FUDGE ...
    PRINCE.
AND IF I DOUBLE YOUR MAGICAL CLOUT —
DON'T HOLD ANY GRUDGE.

    PRINCE and **IL COMPARI.**
MAKE MAGIC, MAKE MAGIC
USE AMULETS AND CHARMS.
    IL COMPARI.
I'LL WAVE MY SWORD AND FIND YOUR LOVE,

AND FILL YOUR EMPTY ARMS.

PRINCE.
YES, WAVE YOUR SWORD AND FIND MY LOVE,
AND FILL MY EMPTY ARMS.

IL COMPARI. But I don't want to promise, Nicolo. Now if you wanted somebody run *through*, well then, no problem, but magic ... it's not as easy as just waving my sword around like some wand.

(He waves his sword around recklessly. In the distance, unseen, CINDERELLA is heard singing, a bit of ì Bells.ſ)

PRINCE. There ... listen! A stray voice in the night! You did it, GodPapa ... a miracle!
IL COMPARI. I did? *Mir‡cola? (He stares at his sword.)* Well ... I don't like to brag, but ....
PRINCE. It's her, GodPapa!
IL COMPARI. Who her?
PRINCE. The very one who was here in the square with us!
IL COMPARI. How can you know? Night voices skim the canals unseen like ghosts. It could be anyone ... or no one ... or even an old monster like I saw here but you didn't.
PRINCE. In my *heart*, I know. Listen. An angel ... a voice smart and loving. The sweet fire in *her* heart knows sadness. A woman, not a spoiled child! I want to marry ....
IL COMPARI. What? A voice? Nicolo ... your father would ... oh, *min‡ccia!* And how could we find ...! You could never ... *impossìbile!* And if you want *more* advice ....
PRINCE. I want *her* as my bride.
IL COMPARI. But ... but ... but ... but ... the ball is planned! Your father says you must choose from the crown princesses of Europe, the Near East, the Far East ... *la luna*, for all I know! Oh Godson, even I, the great Il Compari, cannot work a miracle of *that* size!
PRINCE. GodPapa ... you and I together ... we'll convince my father.
IL COMPARI. *(First agreeing.)* Right, convince ... of what?
PRINCE. Not to have the ball *in* the palace, but *outside* in Piazza di San Marco! Under the night sky! A grand carnival ... with all the unmarried women of Venice ... by order of the King!
IL COMPARI. All?
PRINCE. Every last one.
IL COMPARI. Not royalty? *Ordinary* unmarried women?
PRINCE. Exactly, and to please my father, I'll choose a bride from them.

IL COMPARI. Ah ... well ... that's a relief. At least the King ... from *them*? Not from the princesses?

PRINCE. I will choose only that voice. She is my bride.

IL COMPARI. Nicolo, Nicolo, Nicolo ... how will you know?

PRINCE. Simple ... every woman will sing. A grand idea you had, GodPapa!

IL COMPARI. I? My idea? I didn't ... your father ... well ... sure, I'm known for my brilliant ideas throughout the land. Did I ever tell you about ....

PRINCE. Later, GodPapa. Back to the palace ... to tell my father of your idea!

IL COMPARI. If it's all the same, majesty, I would rather not claim credit ... perhaps we can say ... *you* ....

PRINCE. Don't worry. If there's blame, I'll take it. If credit, you get it. Come, we need a boat. GONDOLA! *(A gondola draws near. The PRINCE listens to the night and calls out.)* Good night, beautiful voice! We will meet again. Dream happy!

(He boards the gondola. IL COMPARI pauses a moment.)

IL COMPARI. I wonder where the old signóra went ... La Stella, did she say?

PRINCE. *(Wryly.)* You mean the *terrible* monster?

IL COMPARI. *(Caught.)* Ah ... well ... *that* ... perhaps only a dream .... *(Sings.)* .
LA STELLA ... *MOLTA B» LLA!*

Laughs and boards the gondola. It poles off. LA STELLA appears.)

LA STELLA. Well ... no matter who gets credit ... it's a good idea. And you're not so bad yourself, Don Compari. Your magic sword needs practice, though. Like you ... it's a little cùculo. *(On the balcony, CINDERELLA hums. LA STELLA listens then speaks.)* Cinderella they call you, eh? All right ... then out of the ashes, we will make fire like stars ... *la Cenerèutola di tuttl stelle!*

CINDERELLA. GodMama ... still here?

LA STELLA. Home to sleep now. Old bones, early tired. Hey, gondola ... come on.

CINDERELLA. GodMama ... is Pulchitruda a witch as they say?

LA STELLA. Only as a drop of water can claim to be the sea.

CINDERELLA. But the *amuleto dfamÙre* ...

LA STELLA. ... She misuses. You *know* the amulet is for hearts to *find* each other, not compel. Good night, child.

CINDERELLA. *Buona nÙte, Nonna.* Keep safe.

LA STELLA. Dream happy.

(She departs in her gondola. CINDERELLA goes for the piece of laundry left in the square. Like the PRINCE, she dances with it then squeezes it into a ball, pricking her finger on a hidden pin.)

CINDERELLA. O-o-ow! A pin! "Find a pin, pick it up
...." *(She laughs.)* Oh Mommá ... finding it in the darkest night must
be *very* good, no? Only *happy* luck for Cinderella now?
    PULCHITRUDA. *(Off.)* CI-I-IN-DER-ER-E-E-EL-L-LAA!
    CINDERELLA. Ah ... maybe not.
    PULCHITRUDA. *Dúrmi*! Early sleep, early work!
    CINDERELLA. *(Looking around the square.)* *Buona nÚte*,
stranger of the night. I hope *you*, at least, dream happy.

(She takes the basket, goes to stairs and sinks down dreamily. Light changes to dream light. VOICE heard in her dream.)

    PULCHITRUDAfS VOICE. CI-I-IN-DER-ER-E-E-EL-L-LAA!

(Shadows, figures, dark sounds.)

SONG: *Demons and Devils and Witches*

ENSEMBLE.
DEMONS AND DEVILS AND WITCHES
TRYING TO TEAR YOU TO BITS,
SCARE YOU RIGHT OUT OF YOUR WITS
AND OUT OF YOUR BRITCHES.
POTIONS, ELIXIRS, AND CALDRONS,
HELLCATS AND BATS IN THE AIR
DON'T DARE TO GO OUT AT MIDNIGHT,
IT'S SPOOKY OUT THERE.

CINDERELLA.
SOMETIMES I HAVE AN EERIE DREAM
OF MOPS THAT CRY AND BROOMS THAT SCREAM,
OF BRIMSTONE FIRE AND HISSING STEAM,
OF GHOSTS THAT HOWL A GHASTLY THEME,
OF SKELETONS AND GOBLINS,
THAT'S A MOB THAT CAN UPSET ME.
AND IF I DON'T BELIEVE IN THEM,
THEY JUST MIGHT COME AND GET ME.

ENSEMBLE.
DEMONS AND DEVILS AND WITCHES

HELLCATS AND BATS IN THE AIR.
DON'T DARE TO GO OUT AT MIDNIGHT,
IT'S SPOOKY AND SCARY OUT THERE!

(A drum sounds distantly and wakes her as it comes closer. PELICULO's VOICE from offstage.)

PELICULO. Stop playing! Clear the way for *un fattorino* from the King!

(PELICULO struts in mightily, tricked out in a stupendous uniform with braid, fringe, medals, gold buttons, a high shako hat, and grand boots. He carries a great scroll along with his drum and is accompanied by a banner carrier.)

Song: Peliculo

PELICULO. *(Spoken.)*
Bang bang bang, bam bam bam
Here I come, here I come, here I am ... here I am! *(Sung.)*
HERE I AM, I'M PELICULO!
I'M THE RIGHT-HAND MAN OF THE KING.
TRA-LA-LA-LA-LA-LI-CULO,
I'M THE BOSS, I'M IN CHARGE OF EVERYTHING!

(STEPSISTERS appear in bedclothes. PULCHITRUDA and PAOLO join them.)

I PLAY SWEET ON THE PICCOLO,
I'M A THUNDERBALL ON THE DRUM.
TRA-LA-LA-LA-LA-LI-CULO,
TWEET TWEET TWEET
DUM DEE DUM DEE DUM DEE DUM

HIS MAJESTY DEPENDS ON ME.
WHEN NEWS NEEDS TO BE FAR-FLUNG,
HIS ONLY CHOICE
IS MY GOLDEN VOICE,
AND OF COURSE MY SILVER TONGUE.

VENETIANS.
HE'S THE FAMOUS PELICULO,
HE'S THE NUMBER ONE VENETIAN DING-A-LING ...
DING-A-LING!

PELICULO and **VENETIANS.**
TRA-LA-LA-LA-LA-LI-CULO

PELICULO. *(Sung.)*
WITH A GREAT PROCLAMATION FROM THE KING. *(Spoken.)*
Gather 'round, listen well
To the news I tell!
Hear ye! Hear ye! Hear ye! *(Reading from parchment.)*
An invitation to all women who are not wed:
Get up! Get out of your single bed
And attend the grandest ball of all!
Tomorrow night —
The grand Venetian wife-hunt ball
To find the Prince a bride!
　　VENETIANS. A bride! A bride! A bride!
　　PELICULO. *(Sung.)*
THE BALL WILL BE HELD *AL FRESCO* UNDER THE STARS
WITH A HUNDRED MANDOLINS AND GUITARS ... *(Spoken.)*
And an accordion! *(Sung.)*
AND WITH A THOUSAND VIOLINS *CON ARCO.*
AND EVERY LADY MUST SING FOR THE PRINCE UNDER
LA LUNA
SO *BUONA FORTUNA*, DEAR HEARTS.
MAY YOUR TONES BE DULCET AND YOUR HEARTS
　　UNBROKEN ... *(Off the parchment.)*
I, Peliculo, have spoken!

(He struts away, stops, decides he's done everything, continues, banging his drum as he goes. CHILDREN ape him behind. Bedlam as the STEPSISTERS shriek with joy.)

　　MOLTOVOCE. A ball! For the Prince to find a bride! And I'm
invited!
　　SEPPIA. I'm invited, too.
　　MOLTOVOCE. But the Prince would be *crazy* to choose you!
You have arms and legs and skin like a squid ... *la seppia!*
　　SEPPIA. Oh ... and you think he'd choose you ... the thundermouth?

(They tangle with each other, considerable hair pulling, slapping behinds, losing slippers.)

　　PULCHITRUDA. Daughters. *(They don't hear her.)* Daughters!
(Still no response.) I SAID DAUGHTERS! *BASTA!* Remember you
are *dame* ... fine ladies.

(They exit. PAOLO sees CINDERELLA below and goes down to her.)

PAOLO. *(Joking.)* With that outfit, why does he need a drum, too ... eh?

CINDERELLA. Oh, Poppa ... I know! And he was more puffed up with himself than with his message!

PAOLO. *Sì Ö un buffÖne.* Listen ... tomorrow I must go to Padua to sell the little saved from my ships. But when I return ... things *will be* different And in Padua, with my last *denaro*, I will buy for you the finest gown ever fashioned in Italy! So ... tomorrow night ... the ball. ....

CINDERELLA. *(Brightly.)* I can go?

PAOLO. Of course, *cara mia* ... the King's great puffing Peliculo said *all* unmarried women.

CINDERELLA. Oh, Poppa, then I'll dance 'til I'm so happy I'll never be sad again! And then I'll sleep and sleep ...

PAOLO. ... until a prince wakes you with a kiss ... like in the stories.

CINDERELLA. Can I always be happy, Poppa?

PAOLO. Breathe.

PULCHITRUDA. *(Off.)* CI-I-I-INDERE-E-E-EL-L-L-LA!

CINDERELLA. If I did get a prince, I'd want one with a soft voice!

PAOLO. *Sì* ... and a warm heart, but most of all ... one good enough for my Angelina ... *la cenerÖntola!*

Song: Unmarried Women

WOMEN.
UNMARRIED WOMEN, UNMARRIED WOMEN,
WE'RE ALL INVITED TO THE BALL TOMORROW NIGHT.
WE'RE OH SO PRETTY AND REALLY WITTY,
THERE IS NO DOUBT THE PRINCE WILL FALL TOMORROW
    NIGHT.
HE'S BEGINNING TO FEEL THE THRILL OF CUPID'S ARROW,
AND ROMANTICALLY SPEAKING, HE DESERVES THE BEST.

(CINDERELLA and PAOLO laugh and dance together a bit.)

I'M THE NIGHTINGALE ... I'M THE BLUE JAY ... I'M THE
    SPARROW.
WE ARE THE FLIRTY BIRDIES HEAVEN-BLESSED.
WE'RE GONNA FLY INTO THE ROYAL NEST.
UNMARRIED WOMEN, UNMARRIED WOMEN,
WE'VE WAITED OH SO LONG FOR LOVE TO CALL
AND ALL OF US ARE INVITED TO THE BALL.
WE'VE CARRIED OUR DAUGHTERS ON OUR BACK TOO
    LONG.

IF THE PRINCE CHOOSES MINE (MINE, MINE, MINE)
HE CAN'T GO WRONG.
IF THEY JUST DISAPPEAR, WE'LL CRY FOR NONE OF THEM,
SO PLEASE, *PER FAVORE,* PLEASE MAKE *AMORE,* DEAR
    PRINCE —
AT LEAST TAKE ONE OF THEM.

(Repeat first two verses.)

*(Light fades. Unseen on the balcony PULCHITRUDA toys with the
    amulet. Music darkens along with the light.)*

END OF ACT I

ACT II

(SCENE: Kitchen. Dawn. Glow from the hearth is the only light. Throughout the opening sequence, light changes, gradually brightening the drop and the scene.
Clock tower chimes behind the action throughout opening sequence.)

Song: *Out of the Ashes / Bring My Porridge*

CHORUS VOICES.
STARLIGHT SLEEPING, SUNLIGHT CREEPING,
OUT OF THE ASHES RISING.
NIGHT DREAMS FADING, DAYDREAMS WAITING,
OUT OF THE ASHES RISING.

(A gondola slides by silently in the morning mist.
A CHILD runs across the square. On the floor at the hearth, CINDER-ELLA wakes, sits up, stretches. She hangs a kettle in the fireplace, stirs the embers then adds wood to the fire and stirs the kettle. She rinses her face at a washbowl and goes to the ì door.ſ)

CINDERELLA.
HELLO, MORNING, NEW DAY DAWNING,
GOD SENDS BLESSINGS FROM THE SKIES,
GOD LOVES EVERY CHILD WHO TRIES.
VOICES.
OUT OF THE ASHES RISING.

(The CHILD runs back across the square, with a loaf of bread un-der his arm. He waves at CINDERELLA who waves back. She stands at the ì doorſ a moment, watching the light change in the sky.)

CINDERELLA.
EMBERS WANING, NEW HOPES GAINING
LIGHT IN EVERYBODY'S EYES.
PERHAPS TODAY THE BLUEBIRD FLIES
TO A PLACE WHERE NO ONE EVER CRIES.
VOICES.
OUT OF THE ASHES RISING, RISING.

(CINDERELLA moves to the kitchen where she sets bowls on the table. Clock tower chimes. A great, dark shadow slides across the room.)

VOICES.
THE WAKING WORLD IS SPINNING
TO A HAPPY NEW BEGINNING ...
OUT OF ASHES ...
OUT OF ASHES ...
OUT OF ASHES ...
RISING.

(PULCHITRUDA enters. She surveys the scene, evil-eyeing CINDER-ELLA who turns away and tends to her business.
Clock tower chimes.
STEPSISTERS enter in dishabille and sit haughtily.)

MOLTOVOCE and **SEPPIA.**
BRING MY PORRIDGE, BRING MY BREAD,
BRING MY FRUIT AND CHEESE.
WE'RE SO HUNGRY WE'RE HALF DEAD,
GET A MOVE ON PLEASE.

PULCHITRUDA.
AND ...

MOLTOVOCE and **SEPPIA.**
WIPE THE TABLE, WASH THE WINDOWS,
WAX THE KITCHEN FLOOR.
CLEAN THE OVEN, SEW THOSE PATCHES ...
WAIT, I'LL THINK OF MORE.

(PAOLO enters, kisses CINDERELLA who continues to tend her chores between the hearth and the breakfast table.)

PAOLO. More what?
PULCHITRUDA. Trouble, of course. You heard, husband, how *your* daughter did as she said ... pushed *my* poor dears in the canal?
SEPPIA. We were sopping wet, stepfather!
MOLTOVOCE. You have to buy us new dresses before you leave. Especially for the ball!
SEPPIA. I want all *pearls.*
CINDERELLA. Poor oysters ... first robbed, then eaten, now insulted.
SEPPIA. Wh-a-a-at?
PULCHITRUDA. You see, husband? Obviously her mother never taught her manners or courtesies.

(CINDERELLA stops cold. PAOLO raises his head and then lifts a finger in warning to PULCHITRUDA.)

PAOLO. No ... nothing about her mother. Nothing at all.

(PULCHITRUDA retrieves the amulet from her bodice, letting it twist above the table. Again light alters, sound of harsh wind, threatening shrieks. PAOLO slumps slightly. With a sudden turn, CINDERELLA knocks a bowl of porridge into PULCHITRUDA's lap.)

PULCHITRUDA. Oh ...! You horrid girl! Look what you've done! *(With another move, CINDERELLA upsets a plate of rolls.)* Clumsy, clumsy fool! *(Making a great display of sponging the porridge from PULCHITRUDA, CINDERELLA snatches the amulet and quickly tucks it in her own pocket. Light restores.)* Get away from me! Leave it alone. I'll tend it myself!

(PULCHITRUDA leaves the room.)

MOLTOVOCE. Honestly, Cinderella. The other day the laundry, and today it's breakfast! You're so clumsy!
SEPPIA. Inherited from her mother probably. *(In a rage, CINDERELLA wheels, lifts a pitcher of milk, pours some on SEPPIA then turns on MOLTOVOCE.)* O-o-oh ... you did that on purpose! Mo-o-ther!

(She runs off, MOLTOVOCE following to escape the same fate. PAOLO follows to calm things down. CINDERELLA moves near the hearth.)

Song: Some Sweet Day

CINDERELLA.
SOME DAY, SOME SWEET DAY,
I SWEAR THAT I'LL GET EVEN
WITH ALL THREE OF YOU.
THEN ALL THE CHORES
YOU'RE ALWAYS TELLING ME TO DO ...
YOU'LL DO, YOU'LL SEE,
YOUR GAME I'LL PLAY SOMEDAY,
SOME SWEET DAY.

SOME SWEET DAY,
I'LL STAND HIGH UPON THIS TABLE,
LOOKING DOWN.

I'LL BE GIVING ALL THE ORDERS,
YES, TO YOU, PULCHITRUDA
AND YOUR TWO PRETTY DAUGHTERS.
YES, I'LL TURN THE TABLES
ALL AROUND,
ALL THE WAY, NICE AND NEAT,
SOME SWEET DAY.

SOME DAY, SOME SWEET DAY,
YOU'LL BE BEGGING ME FOR MERCY
ON YOUR BENDED KNEES,
AND SHEDDING BITTER TEARS.
AND CRYING, "END IT PLEASE!"
YOU'LL TAKE THE GAFF
WHILE I JUST LAUGH,
YOU'LL CRY SOME MORE,
WHILE I JUST ROAR —
I'LL MAKE YOU PAY AND PAY AND PAY
SOME SWEET DAY.

CLEAN, WIPE. WASH, WAX,
MOP, SWEEP, POLISH THE CRACKS.
PUSH, HIT, BREAK YOUR BONES,
SWEAT, STRAIN, LET'S HEAR THE MOANS.
IRON, LAUNDER, SEW, AND THEN ...
DO IT, DO IT ALL OVER AGAIN.
ISN'T IT A FIGHT TO STAY ALIVE?
DO YOU REALLY THINK THAT YOU'LL SURVIVE?

SOME SWEET DAY,
I'LL STAND HIGH UPON THIS TABLE,
LOOKING DOWN.
I'LL BE GIVING ALL THE ORDERS,
YES, TO YOU, PULCHITRUDA
AND YOUR TWO UGLY DAUGHTERS.
YES, I'LL TURN THE TABLE
ALL AROUND,
ALL THE WAY, NICE AND NEAT,
SOME SWEET DAY.

(PAOLO returns, slightly chiding.)

    PAOLO. *Cara mia Ö*
    CINDERELLA. No, Poppa ... *I* will not be *una marionÈta* for them.
    PAOLO. *(Joking.)* What ... Poppa's a puppet?

CINDERELLA. Oh ... poppa ... you can't let Pulchitruda ... GodMama says she is ...

PAOLO. No ... no, not a witch. Sh-h-h-h ... please, no tears sweet one. I said I will do something. I ... don't know what, but I will.

PULCHITRUDA. *(Off.)* She did *what*? That wicked girl ...!

CINDERELLA. Look, I have ...

(She fumbles for the amulet, but PAOLO grasps her hands.)

PAOLO. Come ... before there is trouble again.

CINDERELLA. I have laundry to do.

PAOLO. So we'll walk together.

(CINDERELLA takes the basket and they go to the square.)

Song: Can You Believe It?

VENETIANS.
CAN YOU BELIEVE IT, CAN YOU BELIEVE IT?
I'M ASKING YOU A SIMPLE QUESTION,
CAN YOU BELIEVE IT?
TONIGHT IS THE NIGHT WE'RE WAITING FOR,
TONIGHT LIFE WILL OPEN UP A BRAND NEW DOOR!
CAN YOU BELIEVE IT?
WE'RE ALL IN SUCH A WHIRL.
WE'LL MAKE A PRINCESS,
OUT OF A SIMPLE PEASANT GIRL!

TONIGHT IS THE NIGHT WE'RE WAITING FOR,
TONIGHT LIFE WILL OPEN UP A BRAND NEW DOOR!
CAN YOU BELIEVE IT?
WE'RE ALL IN SUCH A WHIRL.
WE'LL MAKE A PRINCESS,
OUT OF A SIMPLE PEASANT GIRL!
WE'LL MAKE A PRINCESS,
OUT OF A SIMPLE PEASANT GIRL!

CINDERELLA. Oh, Poppa ... I forgot ... you should have seen! Right here ... two nights ago ... a man ... with a mask ...

PAOLO. A robber?

CINDERELLA. Oh, not a *bandito* mask! A beautiful party mask! And a wonderful costume. And his eyes ... even through the mask ... I could see they were soft and ....

PAOLO. O-o-h ... he sounds like a prince! Perhaps Nicolo himself, eh?

CINDERELLA. Poppa! What would Prince Nicolo be doing wandering around our square? No, just a man ... someone I ...

PAOLO. What? Tell me.

CINDERELLA. Sometimes I wonder ... a husband ... children ... a home of my own.

PAOLO. Perhaps your masked stranger will return and take you away from me. To the palace.

CINDERELLA. Poppa ... he was in *costume* and helped me pick up spilled laundry! Does that sound like a prince?

PAOLO. Of the very best kind.

CINDERELLA. You're teasing.

PAOLO. I don't mean to. I wish it were true.

(CINDERELLA dances a few dreamy steps with a piece of laundry.)

CINDERELLA. Poppa ...?

PAOLO. Yes.

CINDERELLA. I think I'm really in love.

PAOLO. Oh, Angelina ... a *stranger*.

CINDERELLA. I know ... a fairy tale. I don't even know his name ... but he was so ... oh, I'm being foolish ... eh?

PAOLO. No-o-o ...

CINDERELLA. Tell me, Poppa ...

Song: Love, Love, Love, Love

CINDERELLA.
IS THIS THE WAY IT FEELS
ALL SHIVERY INSIDE,
ALL WONDERFUL AND TERRIBLE
LIKE ON A SEESAW RIDE.
MY COMPASS DOESN'T WORK,
I CAN'T SEE RIGHT FROM WRONG,
IS THIS THE CRAZY
WAY IT FEELS
THE LOVELY DAY WHEN LOVE COMES ALONG?

LOVE, LOVE, LOVE, LOVE,
I GUESS THERE'S NOTHING IN THE
WORLD THAT YOU CAN QUITE COMPARE IT TO.
LOVE, LOVE, LOVE, LOVE,
IT MAKES YOU DO THE THINGS THAT OTHERWISE
YOU'D NEVER DARE TO DO,
NO, NOT UNTIL A CERTAIN SPECIAL SOMEONE SAYS,

"I CARE FOR YOU,"
WHOSE DREAMS YOU'RE HOPING TO SHARE,
WHOSE LOVE WILL ALWAYS BE THERE
FOR YOU.

PAOLO.
THIS IS THE WAY IT FEELS,
IT'S PLEASURE AND IT'S PAIN,
FIRST ECSTASY, THEN SUDDENLY,
HOT NEEDLES IN YOUR BRAIN.
BLOOD PRESSURE GOES BERSERK,
IT RISES THEN IT FALLS.
TO COIN A PHRASE,
YOU'RE IN A DAZE,
THE LOVELY DAY WHEN SWEET ROMANCE CALLS.

LOVE, LOVE, LOVE, LOVE,
I GUESS THERE'S NOTHING IN THE
WORLD THAT YOU QUITE COMPARE IT TO.

PAOLA.	**CINDERELLA.**
LOVE, LOVE, LOVE, LOVE,	THERE IS NOTHING IN THE WORLD
	CAN COMPARE TO LOVE
IT MAKES YOU DO THE THINGS	IT'S QUALITY
THAT OTHERWISE YOU'D NEVER	YOU SELDOM SEE
DARE TO DO.	IT'S RARE.
NO, NOT UNTIL A CERTAIN SPECIAL	IT'S ONLY WHEN A CERTAIN
SOMEONE SAYS, "I CARE FOR YOU."	SPECIAL SOMEONE SAYS, "I CARE FOR YOU."

PAOLO and **CINDERELLA.**
WHOSE DREAMS YOU'RE HOPING TO SHARE,
WHOSE LOVE WILL ALWAYS BE THERE
FOR YOU.

CINDERELLA. But I'll never see him again, Poppa ... never again. And already I can't remember his voice ... his eyes are fading ... even ...

PAOLO. Then perhaps another. At the ball ... remember? *(No response from CINDERELLA.)* Well, little lovebird ... I'm off to Padua ... but I will return with a gown as I promised. And *then Ö* no more puppet Poppa. *(CINDERELLA nearly draws the amulet from her*

pocket, but doesn't.) Addïo, Angelina.
  CINDERELLA. *Ciao,* Poppa. Safe journey.
  PAOLO. Be happy.

(He watches her from the bridge.)

  CINDERELLA. Be ... happy?

(STEPSISTERS to the square.)

Song: Showoff (Reprise)

  MOLTOVOCE and **SEPPIA.**
FAKER, SHE'S JUST A FAKER,
WISH I KNEW WHAT I COULD DO TO SHAKE HER.
WHO DO YOU THINK YOU'RE FOOLING NOW,
SPILLING A BUCKET OF TEARS,
MAKING THE SOUND OF A DROWNING COW,
WORSE THAN OUR DUMB GONDOLIERS!
DRAMA, CUT OUT THE DRAMA,
SOBBING LIKE YOU MISS YOUR DARLING MOMMA.
TELL THE TRUTH, YOU'RE NOT JUST A PHONY,
IN PLAIN VENETIAN, "YOU'RE BALONEY!"

  SEPPIA. You're in trouble, Cinderella.
  MOLTOVOCE. Yes ... and when you sleep, we'll take your cap and cut it into a thousand pieces and throw them in the canal and then you'll never have anything that was your mother's any more!

(The idea is so shocking, CINDERELLA cannot respond. She sinks down on the laundry and for the first time bursts into tears of total despair. PAOLO makes a sound to get the STEPSISTERS attention. When they realize he has heard all, they flee. As they go, they sing.)

  MOLTOVOCE and **SEPPIA.**
CRYBABY, SHE'S SUCH A CRYBABY,
STUPID CINDERELLA IS A CRYBABY ...

(Lost, CINDERELLA holds the cap and talks to it.)

  CINDERELLA. Oh, Momma ...! I'm so lonely! Is this what I am to be all the rest of the days?

(As PAOLO wonders to himself, CINDERELLA sings from i Hear Us.f)

IF I FLY TO THE MOON, CAN I REACH YOU?
IF WE STAND ON A STAR, CAN WE TOUCH?
You made it happy, Momma ... every day when I was a child, your
little bell song to cheer me up ... I wish ...
    PAOLO. What have I done?

Song: Bells / **Mi Dispiace** *(Iím Sorry)*

CINDERELLA.
BELLS BELLS BELLS
HEAR THEM RINGING ALL AROUND,
RINGING RINGING SINGING,
SUCH A PRETTY, PRETTY SOUND.
HERE'S A BELL FOR DREAMING,
AND HERE'S A BELL FOR LOVE.
HERE'S A BELL FOR WISHING
ON A STAR ABOVE.

PAOLO.
MI DISPIACE, DEAR CINDERELLA,
PLEASE PLEASE BELIEVE ME
WHEN I SAY I'M SORRY.
I FEEL YOUR SADNESS,
SWEET CINDERELLA,
MI DISPIACE
CAN YOU FORGIVE ME?

CINDERELLA.
BELLS BELLS BELLS,
HEAR THEM RINGING ALL
    AROUND,
RINGING RINGING SINGING,
SUCH A PRETTY, PRETTY SOUND.
HERE'S A BELL FOR
    DREAMING,
AND HERE'S A BELL FOR LOVE.
HERE'S A BELL FOR WISHING
ON A STAR ABOVE.

HERE'S A BELL FOR
    WEDDINGS,
BUT MY HEART AND I AGREE
THAT'S A BELL
THAT WILL NEVER RING FOR
    ME.

PAOLO.
MI DISPIACE, DEAR CINDERELLA,
PLEASE, PLEASE, BELIEVE
    ME
WHEN I SAY I'M SORRY.
I FEEL YOUR SADNESS,
SWEET CINDERELLA,

MI DISPIACE,
CAN YOU FORGIVE ME?
I'VE DISAPPOINTED YOU
    MY CHILD
BUT PLEASE DON'T
    FROWN,
THEN CINDERELLA
MY HEART WILL PROMISE YOU
I WON'T LET YOU DOWN.

(PAOLO exits. A distant clock tower strikes the last bong of the hour. CINDERELLA listens sadly. PULCHITRUDA hurries to the balcony.)

PULCHITRUDA. My amulet. I cannot find my amulet! Have you seen it.

CINDERELLA. No, stepmother ... absolutely not.

PULCHITRUDA. Then it must be in this mess you made. *Hunt* for my amulet, girl. Search the floor, search the room, high and low. Find it ... you hear? Then bring it, *directly to* me.

CINDERELLA. Yes, stepmother.

PULCHITRUDA. *(Exiting.)* Well ... start looking. And do that laundry.

CINDERELLA. It's not *your* amulet.

(The NUN and CARDINAL appear.)

NUN. Cinderella, Cinderella ...

CARDINAL. ... you sing like an angel!

NUN. The Prince will choose you as his bride!

CINDERELLA. *(Modestly.)* Oh, no ... I'll be lucky to get to the ball at all. No sooner is one task done than another appears.

PULCHITRUDA. *(Off.)* CI-I-INDER-EL-L-LA-A-A!

CINDERELLA. See?

(They exit separately. PULCHITRUDA and the STEPSISTERS to the kitchen.)

PULCHITRUDA. Where *is* she? Your good-for-nothing stepfather ran off and left us no *denaro* to buy some beauty, so ... we must use what we have. Many preparations, little time ... and she is off doing who-knows-what. We must be beautiful, but if we are too poor to buy ... then we *must* have the amulet, and tonight, one of you must wear it to become the new *principessa*.

MOLTOVOCE. *(Volunteering.)* Me-e-e-e!

SEPPIA. Me!

MOLTOVOCE. Squid!

SEPPIA. Loudmouth!

MOLTOVOCE and **SEPPIA.** Mo-o-o-other ... she's picking on me! Make her stop!

(They exit, tussling. PULCHITRUDA goes to the ì door.î)

PULCHITRUDA. Cinderella! Did you hear me call you?

CINDERELLA. All of Venice heard, stepmother.

PULCHITRUDA. What?

CINDERELLA. Nothing ... I was just ... breathing.

PULCHITRUDA. Yes, wasting time when you should be help-ing us prepare and fix our hair. *S˘bito*, heh? And I *need* the amulet. It's not in my room.

(CINDERELLA goes to the doorway but doesn't enter.)

CINDERELLA. Stepmother ....

PULCHITRUDA. What *is* it?

CINDERELLA. The messenger said ... *all* ... unmarried women. So when I have helped you prepare, then may I get ready my-self?

(Shrieks of laughter, off, from MOLTOVOCE and SEPPIA who over-heard.)

MOLTOVOCE. Oh, yes ... of course ... maybe you can find a gown in the dirty laundry!

(STEPSISTERS, still off, scream with laughter.)

PULCHITRUDA. You? For what? To shame me with your clumsiness and ill manners? Of course not ... you ....

CINDERELLA.'Poppa said I could go. He said he would bring ....

PULCHITRUDA. But ...' *Poppa* ... is not here, now, is he?

CINDERELLA. Then ... the messenger said ... the King com-manded ... *all.*

(PULCHITRUDA sees her dilemma.)

PULCHITRUDA. Yes ... very well ... on one condition.

CINDERELLA. Anything.

PULCHITRUDA. The amulet. Find it ... wherever it's lost. If not, well ... it's not on *my* head then. And take that ugly hat off. It makes you look like ... someone else.

(PULCHITRUDA exits. CINDERELLA draws the amulet from her pocket.)

Song: Amulet

CINDERELLA.
IF I DON'T FIVE THE AMULET BACK TO HER
SHE WON'T LET ME GO TO THE BALL TONIGHT.
IF I DO GIVE IT BACK

SHE'LL LET MY DREAMS TAKE FLIGHT.
BUT WITH THE AMULET IN HER HANDS,
SHE HOLDS SWAY OVER POPPA,
HE CANNOT SAY NOT TO HER COMMANDS.
SHOULD I,
SHOULDN'T I?
IS IT YES OR NO?
WHICH DECISION WILL I CHOOSE?
EITHER WAY, I LOOSE. *(Spoken.)*
Momma ... life gets confusing. Even doing what is right becomes a hard thing. *(She considers.)* It is a trade that is no trade ... as my father the merchant says. *(Decisively, she shoves the amulet back in her pocket.)* No, stepmother ... *(Sung.)*
MY FATHER IS MORE IMPORTANT THAN THE BALL.

(She goes in and sets the laundry basket in the corner upstage of the hearth then sinks down next to it. As light fades to evening, the voice of LA STELLA is heard.)

VOICE of LA STELLA. You have a good heart, *figlioccia.* And a good heart always finds a way. So ... *after* your *O* tormenters ... leave for the ball, we shall see what we shall see.

(STEPSISTERS burst in. They primp and preen in their gowns and sabotage each other's efforts to make themselves at least passably attractive. With a disbelieving look, CINDERELLA leaves them and goes to sit on the bridge steps to anxiously await her father.)

SEPPIA. The messenger said everyone must sing for the Prince. Why?

MOLTOVOCE. Maybe he's starting a bi-i-ig choir. I'll sing something soft and sweet ... a lullaby.

SEPPIA. Your foghorn voice would wake every baby in Venice!

(She imitates a foghorn at the top of her voice. MOLTOVOCE overrides her.)

MOLTOVOCE. "When my squid arms surround you and sque-e-e-eze, You won't even be able to sne-e-e-eeze!"

CINDERELLA. Poppa ... where are you?

MOLTOVOCE. My beauty alone will make the Prince speechless.

SEPPIA. He'll have to cut off his ears to keep his head from exploding!

MOLTOVOCE. Mo-o-o-other! TELL SEPPIA MY MOUTH'S

NOT TOO LOUD! TELL ME THE PRINCE WILL LOVE ME AND
NOT SOME SQUID WITH TENTACLES!
    SEPPIA. Mt. Vesuvius mouth!

(They are at the verge of tussling. PULCHITRUDA enters.)

    PULCHITRUDA. Daughters ... *a la madŪhna*, remember?

(The STEPSISTERS desist in favor of posturing.)

    SEPPIA. Charmed to make your acquaintance, Prince, my name
is Seppia.
    MOLTOVOCE. A *delight*, Prince, I am, the sultry Moltovoce
the Beautiful.

(They realize they have no shoes.)

    STEPSISTERS. Ci-i-inder-e-ella! Our shoes.

(CINDERELLA enters to shoe them.)

    MOLTOVOCE. Don't we have beautiful feet, Cinderella?
    CINDERELLA. Spring blossoms and the scent of the sea, step-
sister. *(Aside.)* Skunk cabbage and dead fish.
    PULCHITRUDA. The amulet ... have you found it?
    CINDERELLA. No, stepmother. I've searched everywhere. Per-
haps Poppa has it.
    PULCHITRUDA. Why would he have it?
    CINDERELLA. Perhaps to sell.
    PULCHITRUDA. Sell! I will make him rue the day he laid eyes
on me!
    CINDERELLA. No doubt of that, stepmother.
    PULCHITRUDA. And ... without the amulet ...

(She shrugs at her daughters in dismay and glares at CINDERELLA.)

    CINDERELLA. I know ... no ball.
    PULCHITRUDA. Then finish your chores since you won't be
going anywhere.
    CINDERELLA. But Poppa ...
    PULCHITRUDA. ... has not returned as he promised ... eh?
    CINDERELLA. *(Disappointed.)* No, he hasn't.
    PULCHITRUDA. *(Triumphant.)* Yes ... not here again when
you need him. *(She gives the STEPSISTERS identical frog-face
masks. Not realizing they both have the same, they laugh at each
other.)* Daughters, pray hard for a miracle. And if he kisses you, re-

move the mask ... become a princess ... as in the stories. *(A clock tower strikes.)* We'll be late. We must hurry.

MOLTOVOCE. We can take a gondola.

PULCHITRUDA. Risk soiling our gowns? The piazza is not far. We'll walk fast.

SEPPIA. Then we'll be all sweaty.

PULCHITRUDA. Then we'll walk slow.

MOLTOVOCE. Then we'll be late!

CINDERELLA. Walk fast and carry a big fan?

PULCHITRUDA. The chores ... the hearth especially, and the amulet! That hat ... !

CINDERELLA. Yes, stepmother. *(PULCHITRUDA and the STEPSISTERS exit. CINDERELLA goes to the i doorf and watches them half-trotting across the square, each with a huge folding fan fluttering. She laughs lightly.)* Like three pirate ships. *Buona fortuna,* Prince ... and beware, fortune is make of glass. *(She eyes the latest mess.)* Mop the floor, clean the hearth ... *(She spots the laundry basket.)* Ö and *still* no laundry done! *(She draws the amulet from her pocket and studies it sadly. Music underscores the following without breaking the action.)* Oh, Poppa ... where are you? What happened this time.

(Voice of LA STELLA in the air.)

LA STELLA. Have faith in the stars, child.

CINDERELLA. The stars are so far away, GodMama.

LA STELLA. But their light gets here ... all the way to the earth, little angel. Faster than I can catch up with my voice. Close your eyes, child, until I tell you. *(CINDERELLA does so. A shower of stars begins in the background.)* Now open them.

CINDERELLA. Oh ... the stars are falling!

LA STELLA. No, just visiting. Now, two spoonfuls of marinara moonlight ... and La Stella is here again! *(Light dims, upstage door of kitchen flies open, mist wriggles in, out of which steps LA STELLA.)* And all in one piece. Hah ... travel by fog! It's nice!

(She is somehow glitterier. She wields a wand which looks like nothing more than a huge wooden spoon. CINDERELLA goes to her.)

CINDERELLA. I'm *so glad* you came to keep me company, GodMama. I'm worried ... Poppa has not ...

LA STELLA. Company? La Stella is never just company, child. And your father's fine. The old horse he hired outside Venice went lame. He's hurrying ... but two legs are slower than four. So ... I've come to help you get to the ball.

CINDERELLA. The ball? Please ... no teasing tonight, I ....

LA STELLA. *(Waving the spoon.)* Hey ... what do you think ... this is just to stir pasta sauce?

(Music under.)

CINDERELLA. *(Skeptical.)* GodMama ... it's only ....
LA STELLA. Hey ... this spoon's got lots more than wood inside! *(She offers the wooden spoon menacingly at the following.)* You want a potion? An elixir? A tap on the behind to behave? *(She taps CINDERELLA's behind jokingly.)* I watch these troublemakers always ordering you around. *Basta dfun pazzo per casa* ... heh? But *one* fool's not enough ... your father brings *three* home ... and the *malůchio* with them. Well, they've been asking for a taste of La Stella's wooden spoon, and now they'll get it. I'm gonna tell them ... listen, you three *ciatroles* ...

Song: *Don't Mess with La Stella / Be Back by Midnight*

LA STELLA.
DON'T MESS WITH LA STELLA, THE GODMAMA OF DEAR
    CINDERELLA.
'CAUSE IF YOU DO,
I'M WARNING YOU ... OOH-OOH-OOH! ...
I'LL DRESS UP IN RIBBONS AND BOWS,
I'LL TELL JOKES AND TICKLE YOUR TOES!
IN MY HAIR, I SWEAR
THAT I'LL WEAR A ROSE
ONE WHIFF'LL REALLY DO YA,
DON'T MESS WITH LA STELLA,
AND STAY AWAY FROM CINDERELLA ...
OR I MAY VERY WELL-A
CAST A HAPPY SPELL-A
ON YOUR UNDERCLOTHES,
AND I MAY POUR A GALLON OF
FUN AND LAUGHTER UP YOUR NOSE!

THE NAUGHTY VOODOO
BAD GIRLS LIKE YOU DO
WON'T STOP MY ANGEL'S CHANCES,
AND HER BIG ROMANCE IS COMING VERY SOON!
TO HELP HER, I'LL MAKE THE MAGIC
FOR CINDERELLA WITH MY SPOON! *(Spoken.)*
So now , wooden spoon, it's time to stir up some *m‡gico*, eh? First things first. Your stepsisters joke about dressing you from the dirty laundry ... no? Well ... a surprise for them!

(LA STELLA stirs the air with her spoon. There is movement in the laundry basket. She stirs harder, and from the basket rises a gown, shedding dirty laundry. It lifts high enough for an astonished CINDERELLA to stand under it before descending over her other clothes.)

CINDERELLA. How did it get in the laundry basket?

LA STELLA. Same way *ricotta* cheese gets in ravioli … a wooden spoon. Easy. *(She reminisces, chit-chatting.)* Whenever I felt the whole world was against me, my grandfather said, "You gotta be kidding, you got *me* to depend on … Severino Says that." It was a game he named after himself 'cause he had lots to say. Well, you, too, child, you got me to depend on. Severino Says. There, all done. And now *scarpe. (LA STELLA taps the hearth with her wand. When nothing happens, she warns the spoon.)* Hey … shoes! *Viéne qua! (In the hearth, crystal shoes rise from the ashes.)* Italian crystal. And like the amulet, good for finding love.

(Dazzled, CINDERELLA puts them on.)

CINDERELLA. Like the masked stranger here in the square?

LA STELLA. Perhaps. But the shoes only *lead* you to where love hides, then your own heart must *find* it. And hear me well … if you do not find the one you love and who loves you … *(Sung.)*
BE BACK BY MIDNIGHT,
BY *MEZZAN" TTE* BE BACK … *(Spoken.)*
… or else the shoes will steal love from your heart forever and leave a lump of hard glass in its place. So … *(Sung.)*
DON'T BE LATE
BY EVEN ONE MINUTE,
OR DISASTER WILL BE YOUR FATE … *(Spoken.)*
… *capiche?*

CINDERELLA. Before San Marco tolls *mezzanútte* … I promise. I *will* find him … I know it. Oh, GodMama, how can I ever thank you?

LA STELLA. Not with tears, child! You'll spot your gown! Now, spoon, how about a cap?

(She taps the basket, rummages in it, and comes up with a beautiful cap.)

CINDERELLA. It's like Momma's … and stars!

LA STELLA. *Sí,* just like my little Giametta's. Now off with you. A special gondola waits … driven by moonbeams. If it must, at midnight it can be back here … *(She snaps her fingers.)* *Ö s˘bito,* like that. *(CINDERELLA gratefully embraces LA STELLA and goes off.)* Ah … so nice … you look like good canoli tastes. *Speciale. (She nods* *approvingly at her wooden spoon and pets it.)* Good work, spoon.

(As light fades on the kitchen, the revolve begins to turn. CHILDREN dance in dreamy slow motion in the square which is filled now with magic light. A gondola 6 canopied, beribboned, and lanterned 6 appears, the GONDOLIER and accompanying MANDOLINIER in splendid white outfits. CINDERELLA boards the gondola which then moves off to one side slowly as the revolve continues and is completed when CINDERELLA is gone.
The square becomes the Piazza di San Marco. Costumed and masked DANCERS whirl by. CHILDREN peek wide-eyed. Music of mandolins, oboe, muted horns.
MOLTOVOCE and SEPPIA enter dancing with the PRINCE. MOL-TOVOCE grabs the PRINCE, embraces him and sings.)

MOLTOVOCE.
DEAR PRINCE, MY SWEET BAMBINO,
I GIVE YOU ALL MY LOVE.

(Her voice cracks on î lovef as a result of LA STELLAfs î wooden spoon magic.î PULCHITRUDA pulls her daughters aside.)

PULCHITRUDA. Never so embarrassed in my life! Why did neither of you tell me you couldn't sing a note? Yowling like stepped-on cats!
SEPPIA. Moltovoce made me nervous.
MOLTOVOCE. No, you made me nervous! I had it *all* planned — dragging him on a romantic walk by the canal, unmasking, batting my eyes at him ... like so .. then leaping into his arms and kiss, kiss, KISS ... Nîcolo, Nîcolo ... ALL MINE! *Then ...*
PULCHITRUDA. Shut up. And you ... tromping on the Prince as if you had eight legs like a squid.

(MOLTOVOCE eyes the PRINCE and makes a slight move toward him.)

PRINCE. No ... no ... no! No more. My ears! My feet!

(PULCHITRUDA pulls her daughters off while casting baleful glances at the PRINCE.)

IL COMPARI. You are not finding what you wanted, Nîcolo.
PRINCE. No, GodPapa, lovely voices, terrible voices. Everything but the one I seek. It is time for another miracle. Bring me my bride.
IL COMPARI. I must be honest, Godson, I think ...

(Halfheartedly, he draws his sword.) … my sword has no magic powers for making miracles.

(He waves it about. At that moment, CINDERELLA appears at the head of the grand staircase and immediately becomes the center of attention.)

PRINCE. GodPapa, look … there is no lovelier vision at the entire ball! Maybe *she* is the one! You did it again! *(Astonished, IL COMPARI studies his sword in wonderment.)* You should never doubt your powers.

(He moves toward CINDERELLA.)

IL COMPARI. Definitely not.

(Impressed, he sheathes the sword with a flourish.
Intent on her search, CINDERELLA has not yet noticed the PRINCE.)

PRINCE. Good evening, signorina.
CINDERELLA. O-o-oh … your majesty? … I'm sorry. I didn't see you.
PRINCE. But I saw *you* and came to claim a dance.
CINDERELLA. Oh … majesty … so many beautiful women … princesses. I came only to find someone … a stranger … but he's not here.
PRINCE. So we both need a partner.

(PRINCE offers his arm earnestly.)

CINDERELLA. Well … yes … then, *grazie.* I'll try to … dance well.

(PRINCE leads her to the center of the piazza as music shifts to a waltz. They dance among the others but gradually, isolate.
Magic light suddenly swirls around the piazza. LA STELLA has arrived at the ball. IL COMPARI spots her and approaches.)

IL COMPARI. Eh, La Stella Volpe … you here? Good costume … you came as … a witch?
LA STELLA. Sure … like you came as what … a *stupido*?

(IL COMPARI laughs.)

IL COMPARI. So what do you think … the Prince will make you his bride?

(LA STELLA laughs.)

LA STELLA. That would be some match, heh? New wine ... old bottle.
IL COMPARI. But you and me ... not so bad.
LA STELLA. Eh ... sure ...

(They begin to dance.)

Song: Compliments

LA STELLA.
YOU'RE ... GRACEFUL.
IL COMPARI.
YOU'RE ... ELEGANT.
LA STELLA.
YOU'RE TASTEFUL, AND MORE.
IL COMPARI.
YOU'RE CLEVER.
LA STELLA.
YOU'RE ELEGANT.
IL COMPARI.
YOU'RE NEVER A BORE.
LA STELLA.
YOU'RE HANDSOME.
IL COMPARI.
YOU'RE RAVISHING!
BOTH.
IN TANDEM WE SAY
YOU'RE MUCH TOO MUCH,
AND WHEN WE TOUCH,
DECEMBER FEELS LIKE MAY.

IL COMPARI.
LET'S DANCE.
LA STELLA.
LET'S DANCE.
IL COMPARI.
LET'S DANCE.
LA STELLA.
LET'S DANCE.
BOTH.
LET'S WEAR A PAIR OF WINGS
AND FLY AFAR ....
LA STELLA.
ROMANCE!

IL COMPARI.
ROMANCE!
LA STELLA.
ROMANCE!
IL COMPARI.
ROMANCE!

BOTH.
THE MOST UNHEARD OF THINGS
ARE WHAT YOU ARE.
ALLOW ME TO CONDENSE WHAT I HAVE SAID ...
A THOUSAND COMPLIMENTS UPON YOUR HEAR!

LA STELLA.
YOU'RE MY CHOICE.
IL COMPARI.
YOU'RE HEAVEN-SENT.

BOTH.
IN ONE VOICE WE SING,
PLEASE HOLD ME TIGHT.
AND OVERNIGHT ...
OUR WINTER WILL BE SPRING!

(They whirl to a dizzy ending.)

IL COMPARI. We make a nice couple ... no? If we ever catch our breath, maybe not only the Prince will find a bride tonight.

(They move aside. Waltz returns.)

PRINCE. You are the best dancer here.
CINDERELLA. Oh ... no, majesty ... I ....
PRINCE. You are, I tell you. I've danced with all. Those two ... frogs. One had more than two feet, all on the left side ... and big. And the other ... *(He points out MOLTOVOCE.)* ... *madonn!* ... like granite! But *you* ... are like clouds riding on air!
CINDERELLA. Thank you. And you as well.
PRINCE. My dance master would be happy to hear you say so.

Song: No One Ever Told Me

PRINCE.
NO ONE EVER TOLD ME
FEET DON'T REALLY NEED THE FLOOR

WHEN THEY ARE DANCING.
NOW I KNOW THEY ONLY NEED THE STARS.

NO ONE EVER TOLD ME
THAT A SONG IS SO MUCH MORE
THAN JUST ENTRANCING
NOW I KNOW IT SENDS YOU UP TO MARS.

(Second time, CINDERELLA also sings.)

IT'S TRUE I NEVER KNEW THE DANGERS
DANCING ALL AROUND YOU
WHEN YOU'RE LOCKED AND BOUND IN SOMEONE'S ARMS.
BUT NOW THAT YOU ARE NEAR, MY
HEART AND I CAN HEAR THE LOVELY SOUND —
OF ALARMS.

(Second time, both sing.)

MAY I TELL YOU BOLDLY,
CAN'T BELIEVE THAT DREAMS COME TRUE,
BUT NO ONE EVER TOLD ME
BUT NO ONE EVER TOLD ME
(First time.) OF YOU.
(Second time.) NO. NO ONE EVER TOLD ME OF YOU.

PRINCE. I believe the Prince has found his bride.
CINDERELLA. Oh ... you flatter ... no, I told you, I came only to find ... but I don't see ....

(The PRINCE interrupts with a short surprising kiss. PULCHI-TRUDA sees, recognizes, then calls.)

PULCHITRUDA. You! How ...? You were *not* to be here! I told you ....

(A clock tower's melody signals the imminence of midnight chimes.)

CINDERELLA. *MezzanÚte* ...! *(Horrified, she realizes she has lost track of time.)* I can't ... stay! Thank you. I'm sorry ... I must go!
PRINCE. But .. you are ... wait!
CINDERELLA. I mustn't! Oh, Momma, don't let my heart turn to hard glass!

(A cacophony of bells. She runs for the staircase and up it, losing a shoe.)

LA STELLA. No child, come back! You found your love! *(But CINDERELLA doesn't hear her which frustrates LA STELLA.)* A-a-ah ... misëria!
    PULCHITRUDA. Ci-i-i-ndere-el-l-la!

(PRINCE pursues but is blocked by the crowd. He finds the shoe on the stairs as the first stroke of midnight chimes. The chimes end as IL COMPARI indicates.)

PRINCE. A *glass* slipper! And *fortune* is made of glass ... as GodPapa always says! I can't lose her!

(He continues after her. The gondola appears and crosses behind. A frightened CINDERELLA is visible. LA STELLA sees her and waves her wooden spoon furiously, but the gondola goes off. On the drop, perhaps an image of a gondola flying. As the revolve begins, lights shift, banners fly out, lanterns die, people move off. Only LA STELLA and IL COMPARI are left.)

IL COMPARI. *Mezzanöte.* Seems the ball is over. Too bad ... too soon.
    LA STELLA. The magic, too. *(Bats the spoon against the palm of her hand.)* Sometimes, it gets stuck in there, gets everything mixed up.

(She raps it again, waves it.)

IL COMPARI. This sword's like that, too. I can't figure out how it's supposed to work. Where are you going?
    LA STELLA. I must hurry ... get things right again.
    IL COMPARI. Leaving? But I ... we ....

(The PRINCE returns, crestfallen.)

PRINCE. She's gone, GodPapa, I can't find her. Come ... we must search all of Venice ... find who fits this shoe.
    LA STELLA. *(Aside.)* She lost a shoe? And he found it? So he has a clue! Not a bad idea ... lose a fly, catch a fish. Perfect ... eh? *(Wiggles an admonishing finger.)* Bad spoon! You like to play jokes ... make me a little *pazza,* huh? But I forgive you ... *if* we set things right.
    IL COMPARI. Majesty ... can't we look in this morning? I must see the *comare* home ... sì, signora?
    LA STELLA. Sure, *now* there's no rush, but it's a long trip ... and your prince says you have to find ....
    IL COMPARI. Your majesty ... we will find her, but first ....
    PRINCE. Then at dawn ... without fail. She *is* my bride.
    IL COMPARI. You have Il Compari's word, majesty ... and his

fierce sword!

(They exit. Revolve completes at the kitchen/balcony set. ì Ashesî underscores. Light colors to day. CINDERELLA, in original clothing, by the hearth. PULCHITRUDA enters to kitchen.)

PULCHITRUDA. You! The Prince is searching the city! He will eventually find his way here. The amulet ... I *must* have it!
CINDERELLA. And I have told you: I don't have it.
PULCHITRUDA. You do. You must. I've looked everywhere except .... *(Roughly, she searches CINDERELLAfs neck and pockets for the amulet.)* Unless you surrender it, I will ....

(She leaves it unfinished.)

CINDERELLA. Put my hands in the fire? No. I'm not afraid, stepmother.
PULCHITRUDA. When your father returns ... I promise you ...
CINDERELLA. ... all will be different. I promise *you.*

(PULCHITRUDA storms off. CINDERELLA exits to the square. She hums and dances a few steps. CHILDREN and NUN appear.)

CHILDREN. Cinderella! Come and play!

(Not hearing, CINDERELLA goes up the steps and off. A gondola nears with the PRINCE and IL COMPARI who carries the glass shoe on a pillow on a gold tray.)

PRINCE. Over half the city, GodPapa, and no one fits the shoe. Perhaps *this* is the square where we first saw her.
IL COMPARI. Those children ... perhaps they know.
NUN and CHILDREN. We know you ... you're ...

Song: The Prince

CHILDREN.
THE PRINCE, YOU'RE THE PRINCE!
YOU'RE THE VERY HANDSOME PRINCE,
YOU'RE THE ONE AND ONLY SON OF THE KING.

BECAUSE YOU'RE THE PRINCE.
YOU MUST LIVE INSIDE THE PALACE
I BET THAT'S JUST THE NEATEST THING.

THERE MUST BE GOLD ON ALL THE WALLS
(AND) SILVER IN THE HALLS
(AND) CURTAINS MADE OF EMERALDS AND CHINTZ.
SOMEDAY WHEN I GROW UP,
I WANNA BE A HANDSOME PRINCE.

(PRINCE and IL COMPARI leave the gondola.)

PRINCE.
YOU MAY THINK IT'S GREAT
TO BE LIVING LIKE A PRINCE
AND TO BE THE ONLY SON OF THE KING,
BUT WAIT, CAN'T YOU SEE
I'M A PUPPET IN THE PALACE?
I JUMP EACH TIME THEY PULL MY STRING.
MY VERY LIFE IS NOT MY OWN.
WHO NEEDS A JEWELED THRONE?
I HAVE BUT ONE DESIRE I'M DREAMING OF —
THE FORTUNE IN MY CUP,
I'D GLADLY GIVE IT UP FOR LOVE.

CHILDREN.
BUT YOU CAN BUY ALMOST ANYTHING,
AND YOU'RE FAMOUS ANYWHERE YOU ROAM.

PRINCE.
BUT EVEN IF YOU HAVE EVERYTHING,
IT'S NOTHING IF YOU'RE ALL ALONE.
HAPPINESS IS ALL THAT COUNTS,
I'LL GLADLY DRINK IT OUNCE BY OUNCE.

YOU MAY THINK IT'S GREAT
TO BE LIVING LIKE A PRINCE
AND BE THE ONLY SON OF THE KING,
BUT WAIT, CAN'T YOU SEE
I'M A PUPPET IN THE PALACE?
I JUMP EACH TIME THEY PULL MY STRING.
MY VERY LIFE IS NOT MY OWN.
WHO NEEDS A JEWELED THRONE?
I HAVE BUT ONE DESIRE I'M DREAMING OF —
THE FORTUNE IN MY CUP …
I'D GLADLY GIVE IT UP FOR LOVE, IT'S TRUE.

CHILDREN.
WHEN I GROW UP, I WANNA BE A
REAL GOOD PRINCE

JUST LIKE YOU!

PRINCE. Now ... since you're all so smart ... perhaps you can help. Do you know who owns this shoe?

(Admiration from CHILDREN but no information. IL COMPARI hands the tray to the PRINCE, and draws his sword. CHILDREN shrink back.)

IL COMPARI. No ... no, don't be afraid. It can't slice even bread.

(He brandishes the sword, stirring the air. Unseen, CINDERELLA sings a few lines from ì Bells.î)

PRINCE. You hear, GodPapa? The same song as that night. *(IL COMPARI brightens.)* That singing ... where does in come from? *(CHILDREN point to the house.)* GodPapa, andi‡mo. Your sword has worked another miracle.
IL COMPARI. Eh ... what do you know? Nothing to it! La Stella was right about how it works!

(He sheathes the sword, takes back the tray, and follows the PRINCE off. CHILDREN follow. CINDERELLA, humming and with MOL-TOVOCE following, enters the kitchen.)

MOLTOVOCE. Are you going to sing that all day? It's so boring. *(A sharp knocking offstage.)* Someone's at the front door. Aren't you going to see who? *(CINDERELLA ignores her and goes out to the bridge.)* Oh ... I suppose I'll have to do it. What good's a servant if you have to do something yourself? *(She goes off. Beat. Shriek.)* Mo-o-other! We have company ... and it's the P. R. I. N-N-N ... T-S!

(PRINCE and IL COMPARI enter behind her. Behind them PULCHI-TRUDA and SEPPIA thunder into the room.)

PULCHITRUDA. Your Majesty ... it is our honor ... had we known ....
PRINCE. I heard ... the voice of my bride. Who sang so beautifully?
MOLTOVOCE and **SEPPIA.** I did!
PRINCE. Oh ... yes ... you were at the ball. The frogs?
MOLTOVOCE and **SEPPIA.** *(Lying.)* Oh ... yes, majesty. But we didn't get to sing for you. There was such a lo-o-o-ong line!
PRINCE. Did one of you lose this shoe? It belongs to the woman I seek.

MOLTOVOCE and **SEPPIA.** I lost it!
PRINCE. Both of you.
MOLTOVOCE and **SEPPIA.** We both lost the same shoe!
PRINCE. Then we must try it on and see.

(On the bridge, PAOLO appears, singing a snatch of Mi Dispiace. *He carries a large wrapped package. CINDERELLA embraces him.)*

CINDERELLA. Poppa! You're back ... at last!
PAOLO. Safe and sound, *cara mia* ... I'm sorry, first my horse, then ...
CINDERELLA. I know ... *Nonna* told me.
PAOLO. You look like your momma with her hat.
CINDERELLA. Oh, Poppa, so much has happened!
PAOLO. Yes ... for me, too. I have decided ... but, no ... first you.

(In mime, CINDERELLA begins to tell him. In the kitchen, the PRINCE takes the shoe from the tray.)

PRINCE. First you.

(SEPPIA sits. She doesn't fit.)

SEPPIA. Well it could fit ... it I trimmed my toenails.
MOLTOVOCE. All the way to the ankles, maybe.

(In the square, the CHILDREN return with the NUN and spot CINDERELLA.)

NUN and **CHILDREN.** Cinderella! What are you doing *here*? The Prince ... he went to your house ... around front!
CINDERELLA. What are you saying?
NUN and **CHILDREN.** The Prince! He has a glass shoe. He heard you singing!

(CINDERELLA and PAOLO head for the house. MOLTOVOCE sits to try the shoe. It doesn't fit.)

MOLTOVOCE. Well, it would fit ... if I ... didn't have ...
SEPPIA. ... feet that match the size of your mouth!
PRINCE. It fits neither, GodPapa! Yet we heard the song! Is there no other in the house?
PULCHITRUDA. None, your highness.
PRINCE. You're sure?
PULCHITRUDA. My most *sincere* word, Majesty. Perhaps ...

their feet ... from dancing ... swollen ...? They were so-o-o-o popular!

(CINDERELLA and PAOLO enter.)

PAOLO. Majesty ... an honor in my home. This ... is my daughter. She has been working hard, as you can see.

(Uncertain, the PRINCE stares at CINDERELLA. A gondola appears with LA STELLA. She steps into the square and goes to the bridge.)

LA STELLA. Now we wait a little bit ... rest. *(She taps the spoon in warning.)* You be good! No tricks!
PRINCE. *(To PULCHITRUDA.)* You said there was no other.
PULCHITRUDA. But a serving girl ...
PAOLO. You call her a serving girl? She is my ...
PULCHITRUDA. ... who cleans and cannot possibly be the ....
PAOLO. *Basta! Statte zitt!* *(He takes CINDERELLA's hand.)* This is *my* daughter! It is more her home than yours! You have made enough trouble in this house ... and there will be no more of it!

(MOLTOVOCE and SEPPIA are speechless. PULCHITRUDA is seething and glares at him.)

PULCHITRUDA. You have my amulet. I want it back to ... *show* the prince.
CINDERELLA. No, stepmother, no spells. Poppa doesn't have it. He once gave it to my mother ... now it goes back to him. From the one place your frozen heart would never dare look ... in fire. *(She goes into the hearth and withdraws the amulet.)* Perhaps you'll find your dreams again, Poppa. *Nonna* says.

(She wipes soot from the amulet on her dress, smudging it, and puts the amulet on PAOLO.
The PRINCE studies CINDERELLA.)

PRINCE. *Saluto!* This *is* the square. The soot on your dress ... blending with the night, you said! It was so dark, but ... it *is* you!
CINDERELLA. You? The masked stranger? I was looking for you at the ball!
PRINCE. *(Laughs.)* And you found him!
CINDERELLA. Oh my ....
PAOLO. You know my daughter? I don't understand, Majesty.
PRINCE. I am here to choose a bride, signóre, and think I have found her.

MOLTOVOCE. *(Bratty.)* She has to try the shoe first … it's the rule.

PRINCE. Yes … you're right. It is the rule. *(He leads CINDER-ELLA to a chair. IL COMPARI waggles his sword furiously, eyes closed, praying. PRINCE tries the shoe, which fits.)* It fits. You have the other?

CINDERELLA. Yes, Majesty. *(She goes to the hearth again and retrieves the matching shoe.)* I saved it … as a dream.

MOLTOVOCE. Oh, sure, she probably fished it out of the canal.

PRINCE. It truly *was* you, at the ball *and* in the square. Your laundry made us friends … no?

CINDERELLA. Yes.

PRINCE. Now will you tell me your name, signorina of ashes on her dress?

(She starts, then with a look of defiant pride at STEPSISTERS.)

> **CINDERELLA.** Angeli … no … I am *Cinderella* Angelina.
> **PRINCE.** And Cinderella Angelina is my bride … if she will be.
> **CINDERELLA.** Poppa?

(PAOLO removes CINDERELLA's cap and brushes a smudge from her cheek.)

> **PAOLO.** You must hear *your* heart, daughter
> **PRINCE.** And what does your heart say, dear friend?

(CINDERELLA studies the PRINCE.)

Song: You Are My Love

> **CINDERELLA.** *(Spoken.)* It says … *(Sung.)*
> YOU ARE MY LOVE,
> MY SECRET DREAM.
> YOU MAKE MY YESTERDAY
> SEEM FAR SWAY … *(Spoken.)*
> Yes.

(On the bridge, LA STELLA claps for joy. IL COMPARI wipes away tears.)

> **PRINCE.** Then … to the palace … to plan a wedding. GodPapa?
> **IL COMPARI.** *Mûta bèlla* … it makes my heart go pitter-pat.
> **LA STELLA.** And it makes this La Stella heart all fluttery …

like little angel's wings!

IL COMPARI and **LA STELLA.** *Che bèlla cosa!*

CINDERELLA. Poppa?

PAOLO. Angelina ... I was late returning ... but I did not forget. I brought this ... too late to be a ball gown, but perhaps it will do for ... you go ... make your wedding. I will stay here awhile.

(CINDERELLA takes the package, hugs him, departs with PRINCE and IL COMPARI who sees LA STELLA and remains on the bridge with her.)

PULCHITRUDA. Paolo ... you'll buy me ....

PAOLO. Nothing, wife. I return empty-handed ... to start over.

PULCHITRUDA. But the *lovely* Cinderella ... a princess now ....

PAOLO. Live off her good fortune? No.

PULCHITRUDA. This beauty ...

PAOLO. ... deserves a glance, nothing more. So, what now, return to Palermo? If so ... eh ... *arrivèderci.*

PULCHITRUDA. Come daughters ... leave everything. We'll soon enough have finer than this poor merchant.

(PULCHITRUDA and STEPSISTERS depart. PAOLO exits to balcony.)

IL COMPARI. I'm tired. I thought magic was supposed to make things easy.

LA STELLA. Hah ... easy like trying to cook ravioli but you don't know how many are coming to eat.

IL COMPARI. Invite me ... then it doesn't matter!

(They laugh. PULCHITRUDA and STEPSISTERS enter the square.)

MOLTOVOCE. It was your fault.

SEPPIA. No, yours.

PULCHITRUDA. Shut up. Gondola!

(At a wave of LA STELLA's spoon, the trio plunges into the canal. PAOLO and IL COMPARI laugh.)

PAOLO. You are naughty, La Stella, to do things like that.

LA STELLA. Me, Paolo? I'm only an old woman with a wooden spoon for stirring pasta sauce ... and sometimes a happy ending.

IL COMPARI. Hah, you have a way about you, La Stella.

LA STELLA. That's what they say.

IL COMPARI. They also say two things make a long life: a quiet heart and a good wife.

LA STELLA. I heard it: a good heart and a quiet husband.

IL COMPARI. Eh'... close enough, huh?

PAOLO. Ah ... my poor Giametta ... how I wish you had lived to see all this. A princess! *(A tiny star floats down and into the hat. PAOLO looks at the sky.)* I'm glad you know. Listen, children ... do you hear it?

CHILDREN. Hear what, Signor Paolo?

PAOLO. Happiness ... *ascŪti.*

(Music begins. The CHILDREN form an aisle for the couple. Grand wedding processional ending with CINDERELLA and PRINCE appearing at the top in wedding garb. Bells resound.)

Song: I Am Your Bride, You Are My Love

CINDERELLA.
YOU ARE MY LOVE,
MY SECRET DREAM.
YOU MAKE MY YESTERDAY
SEEM FAR AWAY.

DUET.
YOU ARE MY STAR
MY BEACON, MY GUIDE
PRINCE.
YOU ARE MY LOVE —
CINDERELLA.
AND I AM YOUR BRIDE.

(Curtain song follows.)

Song: Cinderella

ALL.
COME UP FROM THE CELLAR, CINDERELLA
SHOW THE WORLD THAT UNDER ALL THOSE SMUDGES
YOU'RE *BELLA.*
WARM THE SUN,
BREATHE SWEET WORDS TO THE BREEZE.
ONE BY ONE
CHARM THE BIRDS OFF THE TREES.

THERE'S A HANDSOME PRINCE WHO'S QUITE A PRINCELY
FELLA,
YOU CAN MAKE HIS STARRY SPANGLED HEAVEN MORE

STELLAR.
HE'S CONVINCED NO ONE ELSE BUT YOU
CAN REALLY TRULY RING HIS ROYAL BELL —
IF THE SHOE FITS
WEAR IT CINDERELLA!

THE END

COSTUMES

The costumes should be colorful, whimsical and elegant! The design should reflect all the romance, happiness and magic of Venice, Italy in the style of once upon a time.

SET PIECES AND PROPERTIES

Act I Preset

ONSTAGE INTERIOR – KITCHEN

fireplace stool
fireplace broom
kettle and ladle
scrubbing cloth
table and 3 stools

DRESSING – KITCHEN

2 candlestick holders
clock
dish
statue
fireplace shovel
logs

DRESSING — EXTERIOR

gondola flowers
pots of flowers
window box with flower

Act II Preset

ONSTAGE INTERIOR – KITCHEN

fireplace stool
fireplace broom
kettle hanging in fireplace
ladle
laundry basket
table
glass slippers in fireplace "magic"
one glass slipper preset in fireplace

PROPERTIES

broom
fake fruit basket
shoulder yoke/baskets of fake vegetables
table cloth
basket of fabrics
blindfold
folding stool for Il Compari
Drum with drumsticks for Peliculo
scroll for Peliculo
loaf of bread
laundry basket containing 2 camisoles, 2 bloomers, 4 napkins and lace
concertina
water jug
bread basket
amulet on long chain
large wooden spoon for La Stella
tambourine
bowl of rolls
3 bowls
3 napkins
3 spoons
water pitcher
goblet
wash basin
wash cloth
sparkle wooden spoon
cake
flower basket
masks for ball
fans for stepsisters and stepmother
frog masks for stepsisters
rugged basket for ball gown to fly out of basket
glass slippers set in fireplace
rig ball cap to fly in
star poles for children
lions heads and lanterns on poles — dressing for ball
basket of roses
wedding bouquets

SET DESIGN

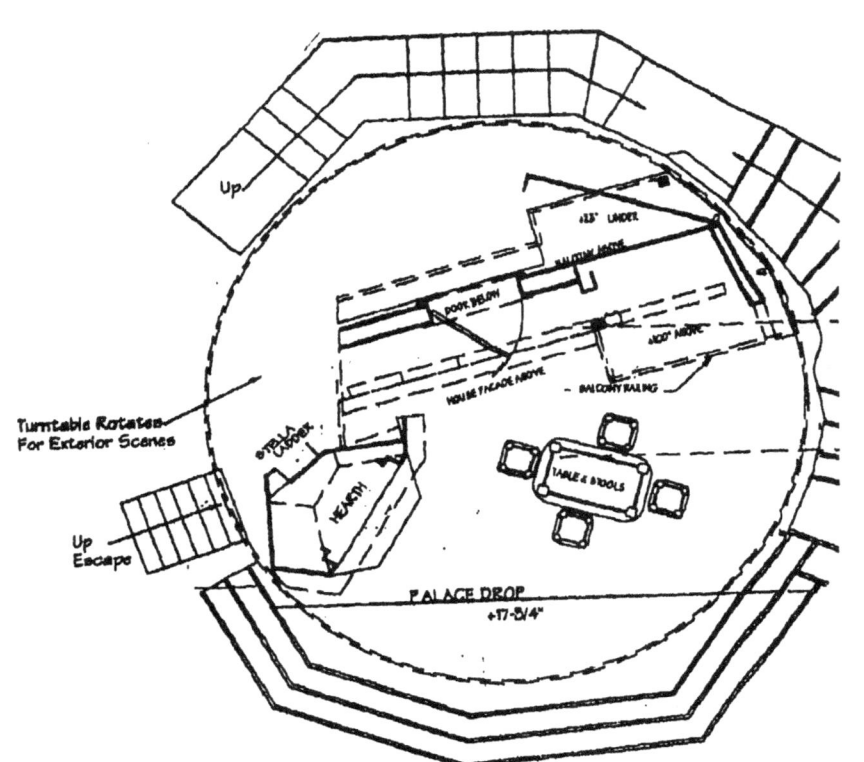

SECRET GARDEN SPRING
Book and Lyrics by Marsha Norman, Music by Lucy Simon
Based on the novel by Frances Hodgson Burnett

Musical / 8m, 7f, 1 male child, 1 female child, chorus / Unit Set

The long-awaited new 70-minute version of the beloved musical is as beautiful and spirited as the original in just half the time. Adapted by Marsha Norman from her Tony-award winning book, it tells the story of Mary Lennox, orphaned in India, who returns to Yorkshire to live with an embittered, reclusive uncle and his invalid son. On the estate, she discovers a locked garden filled with magic, a boy who talks to birds, and a cousin she brings back to health by putting him to work in the garden. The original chorus of ghosts has been replaced with a chorus of Readers, who sit onstage and watch the musical unfold before their eyes, singing in most scenes, and even participating as desired in the storm scene at the end of the first act, and the frolic in the Night Garden. Lucy Simon's music, some of the most beautiful ever written for Broadway, has made this tale of regeneration a favorite for almost 20 years. This new "Spring Version" promises to be a treasure for children and adults.

OTHER TITLES AVAILABLE FROM SAMUEL FRENCH

CHILDREN'S LETTERS TO GOD
Book by Stuart Hample
Music by David Evans
Lyrics by Douglas J. Cohen

Based on the international best-selling book
by Stuart Hample and Eric Marshall

3m, 2f (cast can be expanded) / All Ages / Musical / Unit Set
Inspired by the international bestseller of the same name, Children's Letters To God is a musical that follows the lives of five young friends as they voice beliefs, desires, questions and doubts common to all people but most disarmingly expressed by children. Sixteen tuneful songs and assorted scenes (some based on actual letters) explore timeless issues such as sibling rivalry, divorce, holidays, loss of a beloved pet, the trials of being unathletic and first love. This entertaining show carries a universal message which crosses the boundaries of age, geography, and religion.

As in the best-selling book, the musical is not specifically religious in nature. It's about kids and various events in their lives that lead them to ask a lot of questions – some funny, some serious, some surprising.

OTHER TITLES AVAILABLE FROM SAMUEL FRENCH

TREASURE ISLAND
Ken Ludwig

All Groups / Adventure / 10m, 1f (doubling) / Areas
Based on the masterful adventure novel by Robert Louis Stevenson, *Treasure Island* is a stunning yarn of piracy on the tropical seas. It begins at an inn on the Devon coast of England in 1775 and quickly becomes an unforgettable tale of treachery and mayhem featuring a host of legendary swashbucklers including the dangerous Billy Bones (played unforgettably in the movies by Lionel Barrymore), the sinister two-timing Israel Hands, the brassy woman pirate Anne Bonney, and the hideous form of evil incarnate, Blind Pew. At the center of it all are Jim Hawkins, a 14-year-old boy who longs for adventure, and the infamous Long John Silver, who is a complex study of good and evil, perhaps the most famous hero-villain of all time. Silver is an unscrupulous buccaneer-rogue whose greedy quest for gold, coupled with his affection for Jim, cannot help but win the heart of every soul who has ever longed for romance, treasure and adventure.

TAKE HER, SHE'S MINE

Phoebe and Henry Ephron

Comedy / 11m, 6f / Various Sets

Art Carney and Phyllis Thaxter played the Broadway roles of parents of two typical American girls enroute to college. The story is based on the wild and wooly experiences the authors had with their daughters, Nora Ephron and Delia Ephron, themselves now well known writers. The phases of a girl's life are cause for enjoyment except to fearful fathers. Through the first two years, the authors tell us, college girls are frightfully sophisticated about all departments of human life. Then they pass into the "liberal" period of causes and humanitarianism, and some into the intellectual lethargy of beatniksville. Finally, they start to think seriously of their lives as grown ups. It's an experience in growing up, as much for the parents as for the girls.

"A warming comedy. A delightful play about parents vs kids. It's loaded with laughs. It's going to be a smash hit."
– *New York Mirror*